The Siege of Caerlaverock

Barbara Henderson

pokey
hat

First published in 2020 by Pokey Hat

Pokey Hat is an imprint of Cranachan Publishing Limited

ISBN: 978-1-911279-75-4

eISBN: 978-1-911279-76-1

Interior and Spine Illustrations © Sandra McGowan

Cover Design: Cranachan

Caerlaverock Castle Photo © Gerry Zambonini

Medieval Battle Scene © Shutterstock.com / Zef Art

www.cranachanpublishing.co.uk

@cranachanbooks

cranachan

Based on true events in 1300 Scotland

For my niece Deborah, who shares my love
of the Middle Ages, and of stories.

1

WHERE THE CONSCIENCE COMMANDS

Even though my feet are bare, I feel the echo of every step along the corridor.

Don't drop the candle.

Don't drop the bread.

Don't stumble.

Don't cough.

The wind sings through the arrow slits and I hug my left hand around the tiny flame, pressing the hunk of bread against my body with my elbow.

Back by the Gatehouse, the guards' silhouettes stand outlined in the courtyard. I can't tell which direction they are facing.

No matter, I have to risk it. My conscience commands it.

My skirts flutter around my feet as I duck around the wash-house. I feel the small wooden icon of St Hunna, patron saint of laundresses, bounce on its leather strap around my neck. Fa carved it for my mother a whole lifetime ago. Stooping behind barrels, stairs, sleeping horses and ladders, I run the last few steps and my candle blows out. It takes all my self-control not to sigh with relief as I ease myself through the narrow gap and into the damp blackness of the tower.

I have a little time. Sunrise is still some way off. But how could we celebrate Midsummer Feast with our clan while that poor Squire Colban Graham, lies abandoned in the pit of Murdoch Tower? Lord Maxwell sent the ransom demand weeks ago. Don't his family want him back? A son, sixteen perhaps, strong and fair? I don't understand it.

Step by step, taking care not to knock into anything or to startle the beasts outside, I proceed.

Sir Robert Cunningham would never have allowed a fellow nobleman to be treated thus. But he is not here anymore. I shake off the shiver of memory. Our old Castle Commander is dead, displayed high up on the tower of Lochmaben where he was captured. I wish I hadn't heard the archers talk about it at the feast, but hear them, I did.

Now wheesht; don't cry, Ada. You've a task.

The cold from the stone floor seeps right into my feet, up my legs and through to my forehead and fingertips. Kneeling, I prise the trapdoor open a chink.

'Who's there?' the voice croaks from below. I am

unprepared for the stink: damp, salty, putrid. As my eyes get used to the shadows, I can make out the prisoner's features a little: Colban Graham, a Squire from over the border. When he was led in by his captors, he held his head high, like a man not afraid, when he was not much older than a boy, and terrified, I'm sure.

I hadn't thought about what to say, so I stumble into telling the truth. 'I am Ada. A laundress in the castle, and a friend who takes pity. Here, be sure to catch it. It's not much, but it's from the Midsummer Feast.'

The Squire below me in the pit says nothing. He must imagine his own strong-house, his own kin—his family marking the feast without him. He must wonder why no one has come for him. Maybe he is shocked that he has been here for months already. Moments later, I hear chewing noises, first tentative and careful, then ravenous, like an animal.

'I should go,' I whisper down into the dungeon.

I am waiting for a thank you, but none comes. Instead, there are men's voices at the other end of the courtyard. At this hour?

The horses by the tower begin to shift and stamp. Heavy boots thud on the cobbles. Towards us!

In my hurry to close and secure the trapdoor, it slips from my fingers and bangs shut. *Bangs shut! I need to go, now!* Clattering steps, jerking torches, silhouettes of men—how fortunate that my candle is out, and that I have shrouded myself in dark cloth. The horses know me well enough not to whinny as I squeeze between their bodies and wriggle out at the other end, just as the men enter the tower. I hear the wooden hatch yanked open, squeaking on its hinge.

'The scoundrel is here. He's safe.' The voice is rough and full of rage. 'But how did he unbar the trapdoor?'

'Witchcraft. How else would you explain it, Commander?' the guard answers.

I don't linger to hear more. Hastening along the walkway beside the courtyard is easy; hiding between the brewhouses and sneaking into the kitchen is too, considering I left the door ajar. The dying embers of the fire in the range provide a little comfort and I crouch down. Yonder in that tower, right now, the prisoner will be beaten. I hope for his sake, that someone is on his way with the ransom. But I am glad too. He may be able to bear it better now that he has had some sustenance.

Shrugging off the blanket, I fold it neatly, tuck it under my arm and tiptoe up the stairs, to the servants' quarters. The silence leans on me heavily. In our own chamber, I must arrange my things and hide them under my bed, for fear my father will note the dampness of the night or smell the reek of the pit. I thank the Almighty that he sleeps soundly and use the dirt-rag by the door to wipe out my footsteps as I enter.

I don't know why my heart is so touched by the

4

prisoner. Squire Graham belongs over the border, and we are at war—with his family and with his King, that much I know. They steal our cattle; we capture their sons. Brutal blows and gold. Spiteful strikes and silver. It has always been thus.

Tossing left and right, I try to find rest through the maze of my thoughts, but sleep will not come. War, however, is on the march, they say. 'Tis mentioned in the malt-house, whispered in the stables, mumbled in the chambers above the Gatehouses. They think I don't hear; or perchance, they think I don't understand, but I do. With the rebel leader William Wallace on the run, the English King is bent on revenge—and we on the border are the first castle in his way, a stumbling block to King Edward's plans.

One might think we would prepare—that it would alter our doing in some significant way. But we still seek skirmishes with our neighbours. We hunt and stitch and bake and brew and walk to market. War may come to us tomorrow. Or the King may die, and war may never come at all.

My dreams are fitful and strange, full of salt water and pit-smell, and pain and guilt. Tomorrow is another day. Market day.

A new kind of nausea spreads through me. Confession day, too.

I hardly settle at all until the cockerel crows for the

second time and Fa shakes me hard. 'Make haste, Ada. The Lord is expected back at any moment, and his new wife and the Page are with him. I hear the boy is quite a sight! Make haste!'

Suffice to say, I do *not* look my best when the newlywed Lord and the beautiful young Lady Maxwell ride into the castle. Behind them follows the other fresh arrival—a new Page boy to train. 'Young Godfrey de Heron, they call him,' whispers Mary. Across the courtyard, Brian De Berclay, the Commander, changes his chewed-up mouth into a smile, but it's a false one. His real smile only comes out when he tortures a weaker man than himself.

I've seen it.

My disdain for the Commander must show, for his gaze pierces me hard, even as he waves the Lord Maxwell past and bows. He does not lower his face, nor does he cast down his eyes. Instead, they bore into me.

I'm unsettled. He never acknowledges me.

Why look at me now?

WHY?

He knows. My breathing speeds, my pores moisten and a chill would shake the very core of my heart.

He knows, he knows, he knows.

De Berclay knows!

2

THE CRUELLEST MAN OF MY ACQUAINTANCE

The realisation that the cruellest man of my acquaintance knows of my night-wanderings lands like a punch into my stomach, and I become a little girl again, reaching for Fa's hand. But now that the Lord Maxwell and his new charge have ridden past, my father has already bustled off towards the kitchen—and no wonder. The young wife looks like a gust of wind could blow her away, and a hearty breakfast will be wanted to welcome the new Page boy.

I've seen it since I was little. Rich kin send their boys to become Knights. They begin like this one, Page boys of seven or eight. They learn and become Squires, and if they survive and do well, one day, they may become Knights. I try to imagine the freckled boy with spiky flame-hair on the pony as a Knight, and despite my panic, it makes the corners of my mouth curl a little. He looks like he has been crying. His hair is askew and he has spilt some food or other down his tabard; even from here I can detect the stain on the pattern.

'Ada!' The Steward clips me round the ears for staring. He is right—I will be needed. I will be in trouble if I'm not quick about it too.

Just as I dash towards the kitchen, I risk another look backwards at the guards, talking to the returned Knights. The Midsummer tournament, of course. They fared well, although one reveals a deep cut on his arm, made light of by the others.

Where is De Berclay?

There he stands, aside from the group, running his finger lightly over the edge of his sword—looking straight at me.

I sprint into the steaming kitchen and am glad that the clanging of pots drowns out my panic. Fa's arms are elbow-deep in dough and the griddle is already heating above the fire. He is singing. Always singing.

Until he has something to say. 'Fetch butter, Ada, and cheese. Fetch the new jar of honey, too, and pour mead and ale into those jugs there.'

Mary, the other laundress, is standing by the doorway idle, pulling at her blonde braided loops. Fa groans but says nothing. Mary's sweetheart has returned from the tournament with the Lord Maxwell. He'll be busy disarming his liege now, it's his job remove Lord Maxwell's armour. Nevertheless, Mary is hovering by the door in hope of a snatched word, or a passing touch. I cannot ever imagine being idle like that. My head is heavy with dread, but moving around the kitchen with a purpose helps.

De Berclay and the young prisoner. War and counter-war, feud and revenge. What was I thinking, getting involved? I should have left the young man well alone. But when the Almighty prods your conscience, what can you do? Surely God asks mercy of us when it is in our power to give it?

'Ada, are the sheets dry yet?'

I shake my head.

'Then take the bread to the hall before the family get there, and be quick about it. After that, return to fetch more. You'll need to get to market early, too—the best cuts of meat perish quickly at this time of year.' Fa's hands fly, shaping the dough, cutting and rolling without even looking.

I turn the first batch of bannocks on the griddle, slide them onto a platter and balance the dish of butter and a jug of milk on top. Rushing up the stairs, I wipe a few stray crumbs off the table and place the food at the Master's end. Plates for the Knights and Squires are already laid along the length of it, and I notice a smaller one near the Master for the new Page boy.

Poor child, in his new chamber in this new castle. He must miss his parents, and his wet-nurse too. Maybe he had brothers. Maybe he had a sister just like me.

I stop to listen, but I can't discern De Berclay's rough voice among the chatter. Maybe he has retired to his own chambers, to stare and stroke his sword at someone else. Maybe he has gone to the pit in the Murdoch Tower to torment the prisoner again.

Back in the kitchen, fresh jam boils and bowls of berries and slices of ham sit on the table, ready to be taken up. Still, Mary sighs by the door and I make a point of nudging her with my foot as I speed past again. De Berclay will be seeing to his soldiers by now, surely. Come to think of it, the Lord Maxwell will want a word with his Commander. Following the tournament, there will be news, there will be instructions. He'll be too busy to think about me, won't he?

My own instructions come without delay. Fa wipes his hands on his apron. 'Ada, here be some silver from the Stewart. Go to confession as usual and then fetch the food from market as I told you, before the sun gets too high.' He pours the words out as if he was already hours behind—just the reason why the Maxwells value him so much, I think. My father isn't late for anything, ever. Sometimes I wonder that I am his daughter at all.

I tuck the small bag of silver into the basket, press down the false wicker floor and place another bag with just a single piece of silver on top, just as Fa taught me. That way, if Reivers attack, they may be fooled into not taking all I have. Putting on Mary's old boots for the journey, and wrapping a long shawl around myself, I cross the courtyard.

The guards have lowered the drawbridge already, and some of the Squires are training just outside the moats in the distance.

I hadn't realised how tense I had been, but there is no sign of the Commander, and I'll be out of the castle all day. All will be well.

I round the East Tower and the guard chamber, whistling, and am about to step out onto the bridge when a big, cold, hairy hand claws into my hair and pulls me backwards. A second cold hairy hand closes around my throat, and I feel the prickly stubble of the Commander's beard scrub against my cheek.

3

CONFESSION

Even if I had wanted to, I don't think I could have screamed. He drags me backwards towards the shadows of the portcullis slit where we cannot be observed by those within or without.

I don't struggle. I have seen this man hurt children and animals. If I don't struggle, I may make it to confession. But just in case I don't, I say a prayer in the privacy of my mind, in the hope that the Almighty listens to girls in distress.

De Berclay's hand around my neck loosens a little and his nose approaches my ear. I feel faint. Is he going to throw me into the moat? Beat me? Is he going to tell the Lord Maxwell that I have disobeyed and helped the prisoner?

'Listen, girl.'

I can't speak.

'I've been told you're going to the burgh. I need you to

do something for me. Take this.'

He pushes a letter into my hand.

'This must be placed int' the hands of the Toll Master at Dumfries, do you hear?'

I am still frozen.

'*Do. You. Hear?*' He doesn't shout it—it's a whisper still, but a hiss more terrifying than if it had come from the devil himself. I nod, struggling against the pressure on my throat.

'Yes, sir,' I manage to croak and he drops his hand from my neck.

'I know you're a good, godly girl. A sensible girl. So, hear this: if you tell anyone about this letter, I will kill you.' He says it slowly, calmly, but his eyes are unblinking. He smiles a mouth-only-smile and I flinch.

With the vice grip gone, I am free to run. And run I do, sprinting across the drawbridge with a clatter of steps and swinging my basket behind me, only just holding on to the shawl. I race along the road, past any fellow marketgoers, and at Glencaple a fisherwoman offers me a ride on her cart. Watching the crows circle overhead, I allow myself to think about what happened. *The letter!*

I reach inside the basket and close my clammy fingers around the folded parchment.

It bears the Lord Maxwell's seal.

The Lord Maxwell's seal? But this is not how the Lord Maxwell does business! Not secret and sinister.

Surely the Lord would send a proper messenger, not a laundress. Does my Lord know of this?

He must do, how else would the sealed letter come into the possession of such a man as Commander De Berclay?

Not long before we reach the gates of the Burgh of Dumfries, the fishwife turns. 'Get off here, lass. They're suspicious of us all, and I certainly won't vouch for you.'

She waves her hand dismissively and I grab my basket and slide down onto the dusty road. 'The Lord bless you for your kindness, guidwoman.'

She waves curtly and approaches the burgh gate where her wares will be searched. An official puts out his hand for the toll without even looking at me. I stand and wait until he glances down, though he looks far from pleased. 'Yer toll, lass and begone with you.'

'Pardon, sir, but I need to speak with the Toll Master.'

His forehead furrows. 'What about?'

'I'm not at liberty to say, sir.'

I bow my head politely, hoping that his displeasure will not result in my being barred from entering the burgh at all. A couple of gaberlunzies are taking an interest, waving their empty purses at me as if I was a nobleman's daughter.

'The Toll Master is busy. Off with you.' He shoves me back and allows some other sellers and buyers to pass, with ingots clinking into his collection bag.

'Very well,' I answer as soon as there is a lull of arrivals. 'I have a letter.' I hold it up only long enough for the seal of the Maxwell family to do its work. The official blanches, takes a step back and makes a mock bow.

'I'll see that he gets it,' he snaps, reaching for the letter. I snatch it away only just in time.

'I have been expressly told only to put it in the Toll Master's hands,' I wince, but he doesn't strike me—for fear of my Lord Maxwell, I suppose.

'What is it? Who asks for me?' The Toll Master is a small, weedy man with jet-black hair and a hat much above his station. But unlike his official, he is quick. 'Give me that!' he sneers, slashing the parchment out of my hand and making off towards the Toll House with it. I take my chance and run, ducking through the Toll Gate with a passing crowd and ignoring the official's demands for payment which cease almost immediately.

More has happened in the last ten hours than possibly in the whole of my life put together. I need to think. I need to rest. I need to figure out what in the world is going on.

But all of it will have to wait until I have made my confession.

The stout churchman at Greyfriars Kirk is just bidding an old carlin wife *Godspeed*. He drops his manuscripts when he notices me standing there, dishevelled and panting, still pressing the basket to my chest. His papers have sailed to the floor. One particularly richly illuminated sheet lands on top of his sleeping dog, curled up below the baptistry. He makes light of it.

'Nosewise sleeps through anything! He is the laziest dog I know. But why so frightened, lass? You're from Caerlaverock, are you not?'

'Yes, Friar Malcolm.'

'A servant?'

'A laundress. And I help in the kitchen too. My father is the cook there.'

'Ah.' Understanding spreads over his face, but no condemnation. The story is old, and everyone in these parts knows it. Eight years ago, my mother died giving birth to my brother. It pleased the Almighty to take both of them from us that day. That is all there is to it. If it hadn't been for the Lord Maxwell, I might have been sent to the alms house, being a useless girl of four, but Fa is a worker—the hardest worker I know. Lord Maxwell allowed me to stay, out of respect for Fa.

Sometimes I wonder at the way my father looks at me, with such loss etched on his face. *'You look more like her every day.'* There is love in his voice, but I'm not sure it is for me. His arm muscles tense and he rolls up his sleeves for the next task, wiping his forehead only briefly before the task after that. On and on, until he is so exhausted that he doesn't have to feel. Sleep claims him the moment he sinks onto the straw mattress in our small servants' quarter.

The Friar points me to the confession booth. He knows who I am now; I know who *he* is, and yet we pretend to be strangers. I confess to hunger and greed, to laziness and to coveting Mary's new sash. I confess to doubting and arguing and a fit of temper a couple of days before the feast.

Of the prisoner, and of the letter, I say nothing.

I hang my head, make the sign of the cross, and close my eyes.

The Friar looks at me. 'I sense burden. I sense you are bearing secrets that are not yours.'

Can he read my mind?

Deep breath.

Make light of it, it's the only way.

'I have plenty burdens of my own, without worrying about others,' I smile.

He acknowledges this by inclining his head and busies himself with his papers until his little dog barks and he nearly drops them again. Nevertheless, I can feel his eyes boring into me as I leave confession booth and make for the door, carefully side-stepping the burial stones of various Maxwell Lords in front of the altar.

Who is going to pray for my soul when the time comes?

If De Berclay has his way, that time might come soon. My body will be in a ditch.

He won't want any witnesses, whatever he is up to.

And the Commander is up to no good, of that I am sure.

4

THE MERCAT CROSS

The market in the burgh wipes out my worries like the sky clears after rain. Stalls, trestles, sellers and carts, as well as the guild wares, line the street. Horses and donkeys weave through the throng and callers compete on every corner, be they beggar or bard, sometimes both. Stories are told, ballads are sung, silver pieces skip from one hand to the other. People from far and near come to Dumfries on market days, but even more than usual have come today. Of course, everybody needs to replenish their stores after the feast.

'Ada! Hither!'

My father's favourite flesher waves and I collect the first order, burying parcels of meat deep in the basket. Bread and cheese follow, along with new candle wax and spices, and some leather off-cuts for the repair of shoes. Soon, my basket is heavy, but there is nothing I can do about that. Balancing it carefully with both hands, I strap it onto my bent back and re-enter the fray, slowly edging my way along—when it happens.

I'm not sure how I know it's significant, or how anybody else knows either. A horse's hooves pound the ground, even though dozens of horses have made their way past already. A shouting voice among the hundreds of shouting voices, and yet, somehow, one by one, we fall silent.

'Tis a messenger, but not the usual Herald. I've never seen his horse before either, a distinctive chestnut-and-white piebald—the like of which we rarely see in these parts. He comes to a standstill at the Mercat Cross and faces the crowd. His horse is sweating. He has news.

We wait.

He remains silent until someone throws him a bag of coins. It falls to one of the Burgesses to pay, a proud merchant. 'Out with it, man—what news?'

The Herald takes his time to check the contents of the clinking bag, and a couple of impatient, well-dressed men at the front throw him more, the coins landing at the feet of his horse. He leans to see but doesn't dismount to pick them up. Stretching high in his saddle, he shouts out his news as a proper Herald does, with his eyes half closed.

'The King of England, Edward Longshanks, is making ready for war on this border.'

There is an audible gasp, and a commotion in the

crowd. I am knocked leftwards with my basket and struggle to steady myself, so heavy is my load.

The Herald continues: 'The King made ready at Carlisle on the day of St John's Feast and will reach these lands in days. He means to defend his name as Hammer of the Scots. They say he has more than a thousand men. Some say as many as three thousand.'

Some of the sellers have begun to pack up their wares. The sharp-witted people in the crowd rush to trade quickly, before the opportunity is gone, clutching armfuls of supplies, just in case. *Should I?*

But then I realise that I have spent our silver, and what can one girl do in any case? I can't carry enough for a whole garrison of soldiers, can I? I can only hope that the seat of the Lord Maxwell is not worth bothering with, out of the way by the sea and away from important burghs such as Berwick and the like.

'You have been warned. Make ready; make fast your homes and defend your land.'

There are conflicted faces all around, especially from those who swore fealty to the English King only a few short years ago, our last Lord Maxwell among them, God rest his soul. With no King in Scotland, our clan decided to take a chance on William Wallace soon afterwards. But now? Where to place one's loyalty? Where to deploy one's men? In these Borderlands, the key to survival is backing the winners, whoever they may be.

Why am I bothering with these questions, being nothing but a laundry girl? I feel my heart plummet. My Lord Maxwell must be told as soon as possible. He will know what to do. He will take command, and if he has any sense at all, he will send De Berclay back to the slimy hole from whence he came.

The Herald waits while his horse swishes its tail. More well-to-do women approach him and entreat him to say more, slipping coins into his greedy hands in exchange for whispers, whether true or not is anyone's guess.

But I have heard enough. The whole market square is on the move—packing, shifting, carrying—then dissolving across the bridge and onto our own separate paths. No one thinks to offer me a ride this time. Horses trot smartly past me and carts clatter to the shore. I half-walk, half-run, glad to have my purchases at least. They are weighty, but the news is heavier. Beside me on the right, the calm glow of the Solway Firth contrasts sharply with the frantic activity on the roads and with this new torment in my soul. There are many people, but few words. What is there to say? A hush settles on the road, as if our secrecy could avert an English army or dissuade their King. Thinning with each passing village, the crowd turns into a handful, until there is only me, alone with the reddening sky reflected like an omen on the western waters.

I pray, silently, for this cup of suffering to pass us

by. How hard it must be to be a master, the one who decides what to do and what to leave undone, to fight or to submit. My thoughts turn to the Knight William Wallace who led the Scots in such a victory when I was very little. There was hope then. Now he is in hiding and there is no King in these lands, and all the border families fight amongst themselves, changing sides like the wind blows east and west.

We are not ready. I have no military mind, but our castle barely holds out against our own enemies, never mind an English army of hundreds, maybe thousands. I feel alone with the news, but the thought of sharing it is worse.

The last, uphill stretch to the castle is hardest. I turn right off the road where it sits, unsuspecting and still. The moats reflect the burnt sky, circling Caerlaverock like a fiery target. All around, singing skylarks shoot up into the summer air like sparks.

I swallow, wiping my clammy forehead with clammier fingers.

Arriving means telling.

Telling will make it true.

And what happens then?

5

THE HEDGEHOG

The drawbridge is still down, but the guards are not even paying attention as I shuffle through, my feet like lead weights. Instead, they are playing with the new Page, allowing the wee boy to handle a broadsword almost twice his height. The boy takes it, struggles to hold it upright, staggers a little to the left, rights his footing and lifts the sword high above his head. Old Sir Walter Weir, the Depute Castle Commander, is motioning towards his long white beard in jest, and the Page boy tries to cut it with the broadsword. It looks like that weapon is wielding *him*, not the other way around. The old man's ready laugh echoes back from the castle walls, while the Page boy frowns in concentration, trying to keep his balance.

The rest of the guards roar with delight, clapping and patting him on the back. The young boy smiles a little uncertainly at Sir Walter.

No one pays me the smallest heed. De Berclay, mercifully, is nowhere to be seen.

The evening stew is already cooking over the range and Fa is taking a rare moment to relax by the glow of the fire. It always surprises me how he reads me. He is on his feet like a whip.

'Ada, what is the matter?'

I lower the heavy basket on the floor. *How can I begin? The prisoner, De Berclay and now this, worst of all!*

He misinterprets my hesitation. 'What did the Friar say at confession?'

He thinks my conscience is troubling me.

Maybe it should.

'Do not worry, Fa, the Friar absolved me. But Fa, there was a messenger bringing news of the border. There is an army.'

He shakes his head, as if that could avert it.

'Truly!' I cry. 'Coming over the border, and soon. The King himself is leading it, the Herald said, and they have gathered at Carlisle. They are surely coming. The Lord Maxwell must know of it as soon as possible.'

That is the point at which I have done all I can do. Suddenly, I feel the pain on my shoulders where the straps of the heavy basket cut in. Suddenly, I feel the rumble of an empty stomach, the rasp of a dry throat. I sway.

Fa pushes me down on the bench. 'I'll send for the

new Commander. De Berclay will know what to... What is it, Ada?' The vehemence of my raised hands has made my fear plain.

'Not him.' I croak. 'Anyone but him.'

Fa gives me a sharp look and rushes out of the kitchen. Before long, I am relaying everything I know to Old Sir Walter Weir. He has been one of the Maxwell Knights for longer than I have been alive and is a favourite of my father's. He treats Fa with respect, despite our low status. He nods thoughtfully and strokes his beard without interrupting until I am finished, and I trust in the wisdom of his advanced years.

'Thank you,' he says simply, and disappears in the direction of the Gatehouse where the Lord Maxwell is resting.

He won't be resting for long.

Just as I predicted in my thoughts, shouts ring out in the courtyard a mere half an hour later. Despite my task of boiling the shirts soiled by the Lord's last journey, I can't resist running to the kitchen door every few minutes. The horses are already saddled, including the Lord Maxwell's black mare. A Squire comes into the kitchen and asks for a clutch of saddlebags to be filled with supplies.

Fa nudges me not to stare, bending down as he slices the cheese. I wander listlessly back to the wash-house.

The next time I peek through the door, the Lord

Maxwell is speaking to some of his best warriors. De Berclay is there too, nodding and looking serious. *Please, let the Lord Maxwell take that man with him.*

I nearly drop the soap bar I am clutching. 'Mary! Look! Our Lord Maxwell is handing De Berclay the huge iron keys to the castle gates! Does he mean to leave him charge again so soon?'

Mary nods. Her eyes are watering, for her sweetheart is to be one of the party again. 'They are riding out to consult with the allied clans on how to proceed. They are sure to be back before the English army get here, he told me.' She sighs and wipes her cheek with her apron corner before repeating '*they are sure to be back*', more to herself than anyone else.

There is running and shouting, fetching and bringing, and the Lord Maxwell himself gives instructions to keep the bridges pulled up and the portcullis down—unless we can be certain of no threat.

The Lord Maxwell swings himself into the saddle. With his lance, sword, chainmail and plates, he looks like he is riding out to war, not to a council. Mary's Squire nods in farewell as they ride past. High on the battlements, the Lady Maxwell's dress blows in the wind, and she insists on standing there until our men's party has disappeared over the darkening horizon, no matter how hard her maid pleads with her to guard her health.

I think about a thing the Friar from Greyfriars Kirk

said at the beginning of my confession. *'The soul is attached to the body only by a fine thread which can sever at any moment.'*

How many threads will fray and tear in the days to come? I must make ready for eternity, I suppose. Turning to see whether Fa or Mary are looking, I step into the kitchen and slide another hunk of bread into my sleeve, adding some cheese into the other.

'What are you doing?'

I jump so violently that I collide with a pan hanging from the rack. It clangs into the pot next to it, and that swings into another. I am so swift to stretch my hands out to stop the noise that I knock an earthen jug of cream to the ground where it shatters on the flagstones. Shards and cream slosh around at my feet and I look in rage at the boy in the doorway. The new Page boy.

'What are you doing?' he repeats, with reddened eyes.

'None of your business.' I glare back.

We stare at each other, but my heart softens a little. He has been crying, I am sure of it.

'Godfrey is my name.' He still stares at my sleeves.

'I know. I'm Ada, and I am busy!' I snap and turn my back to wipe up the cream, in the hope that he will go away.

He doesn't. Fa is looking out ingredients in the scullery and Mary is in the wash-house. But this boy is not so easily shaken off.

28

'I saw what you did,' he says, not bothering to keep his voice down.

I cough to mask his voice. '*Wheesht!*' I hiss with a warning look, glancing briefly across to the scullery.

'I said, I SAW what you were—' he begins, louder. He means to force my hand, and what's worse, his gamble is working. I have no choice but to rush to the door, put my arm around his shoulders and guide him away from prying ears. Once we are clear in the corner of the castle courtyard, I wheel round.

'Good sir, you may be new here, but you have no right to wander into the kitchen like that.'

'I'm certain that *you* have no right to steal the Lord Maxwell's food. You're only a laundry maid,' he sneers.

It would make a Pope laugh: He is more than a head smaller than me, and his hair stands upright like a hedgehog, and yet he knows of the power he has over me.

'Keep your voice down, prithee,' I spit. 'I'm not stealing. I'm only making sure that all Lord Maxwell's… guests… are provided for.'

'By putting food up your sleeves?'

'Keep your voice down!'

He grins. 'Confess everything or I'll tell. The Lord Maxwell's Commander will be interested, will he not?'

My stomach twists like fine yarn and my eyes blur. *Would this whelp tell De Berclay?* I scrutinise his freckled face and his spiky hair. His eyes don't even blink. *Is he completely moonstruck?*

I'm a fine one to talk! What could be more moonstruck than taking an eight-year-old stranger into my confidence? I must be mad! I hate myself for even considering it, but there is no choice.

The corners of his mouth curl up.

No choice at all.

And he knows it.

6

A NEW ALLIANCE

I am still questioning my sanity when I sneak down the servants' stairs and step out into the moonlit courtyard a few hours later. The guards are not distracted now— the news from over the border has done its work and even in these early hours of the morning, they stand on the battlements, narrowing their eyes into the distance, keeping their bows strung and their lances sharp. Listening into the night-still air, their attention is on the threat outwith the castle walls, not on the culprits within.

I can't decide whether I *feel* guilty or not. It's not so very bad to bring a young and abandoned prisoner some sustenance, but shame gnaws at me for stealing, and for telling too. Silly wee rich boy, sticking his nose into matters that do not concern him! I sigh deeply as I tiptoe past his chamber, making the agreed signal—a slow scratch along the wooden door with my fingernail—a knock might startle those sleeping nearby.

He'll have fallen asleep, I think hopefully. Maybe he has lost interest in the prisoner and allowed himself to be lulled to sweet dreams instead.

There is no sound from within the chamber. I count to ten, slowly. No. He is not coming. My heart skips inside me. Maybe he'll even have forgotten by the morrow. My stomach, strung tightly, begins to ease. All may not be lost. He is only a boy, a young one at that, and boys flit from thing to thing like grasshoppers. I won't be of interest to him on another day; he'll simply find another unsuspecting soul to torment in his boredom. For now, I can concentrate on getting to the prisoner unseen.

I am only just realising how tense I have been and sink against a pillar with a sigh of relief—which is when I feel the chill of an icy blade against my throat.

'Well, well, well,' the dreaded voice mutters. 'Who has been all but invisible today then, hmm? One could almost imagine you had been… avoiding me.' The beard again, stabbing into my cheek. De Berclay strokes his sword without removing it an inch from my neck. I can't even bring myself to swallow, so dry is my throat, and a croak emanates from it involuntarily.

I sound pathetic.

I am pathetic.

'Now, girl, I need you to tell me that you passed on my letter, as I asked you.' His voice is low and smooth, as lifeless as a frozen loch. I picture my own lifeless body floating face down in the moat. This man is the one to make it happen. He has the power, and no one would ask questions. As Commander, he would be in charge of any investigation anyway. *Think, Ada, think!*

'Did you?' He almost sings it.

'Yes.' I squeak, as nodding would result in cutting my throat on his blade. 'Sire,' I add. But politeness is wasted.

'Now, these dealings betwixt the Toll Master and myself are private. Very private. But since I was prevented from attending my meeting with him in person, I had to send you. You saw the letter, did you not?'

This time I assent a little too quickly, before realising it is a trap. My *yes* is my death warrant.

'I… regret… that you saw the seal, little girl, I really do.' He casts his eyes down in mock distress, but he will murder me for knowing of his deception, and I am powerless to stop him. *Oh, Almighty God, at least I was at confession today. Oh Heavens…*

Creeeak.

We hear a mighty yawn, see an open door and the Page boy called Godfrey appears, staring wide-eyed at the Castle Commander and his gleaming weapon.

De Berclay's sword clatters to the ground where Godfrey picks it up and offers it back to the Commander with both hands without missing a heartbeat. 'Sire, I beg your pardon. I did not mean to startle you.'

I ease myself away and watch the Castle Commander struggling for words. How could he possibly explain his actions? But I am so over-filled with fear that it is bound to rip through me and spill out. I can't think of anything except standing rooted to the spot.

'Come, maid,' the boy insists as he nudges me towards the open door of his chamber. 'You brought the bread as I asked, did you?' I can only nod. De Berclay opens his mouth but Godfrey is quicker. 'Boys like me are often hungry, you see. But I'm fearful of waking the Lady Maxwell with our idle chatter. Goodnight, Commander De Berclay.'

He shuts the door behind us and I don't resist, clutching my throat and holding my breath so I do not have to inhale the same air as that monster.

Sitting cross-legged at the foot of Godfrey's bed, I unburden my beleaguered soul and whisper of my fears and failures, of the underhanded use of the Lord Maxwell's seal and of the cruel treatment of the prisoner in the tower. For a boy so young, Godfrey understands quickly and grasps the full scale of our challenge. For a boy, he is also not so very terrible at listening to a girl.

When I say so, he smiles. 'Five sisters,' he shrugs and for the first time that night, I manage a laugh. We peer out of his draughty window and see De Berclay walking back to his own quarters across the courtyard, taking his murderous intent with him. We watch a candle flicker at his window. A short while later, the light goes out.

Moments afterwards, we tiptoe slowly across the walkway, down the creaking steps past the horses who snort dreamily, and into the Murdoch Tower, lifting the trapdoor gently. Beneath us in the gloom, all is still. However hard I listen, I can't detect a sound. I open the trapdoor a little wider and peer into the pit.

There is a small adjustment of step below and I shrink back, before remembering that no man, however young and agile, could possibly jump up to the height of the trapdoor.

'Are you there?' I ask, as if he could be otherwise, other than dead. I nod to Godfrey to open the hatch some more. No answer.

'I've bread and cheese for you.' Once my eyes have adjusted to the low light, I can just about detect an outstretched hand below us. Godfrey wrinkles his nose. 'Are you sure this is a person and not a pig?' he whispers, and I elbow him for fear Squire Graham might hear.

'It's not his fault. He was captured during the Lochmaben attack.' I hiss back.

Below us, the prisoner is eating audibly now, and I feel a little bit better. Bringing bread to the hungry is surely my Christian duty, which I have now discharged. My heart goes out to him down there, with the smell and the rats. The dark.

'Why won't you speak?' I whisper down. 'It's Ada.'

Suddenly, without warning, a hand appears on the rim of the opening, though I have just declared it impossible, and I stumble back with a stifled shriek. Godfrey loses his balance and topples backwards, dropping the heavy hatch which crashes down onto the prisoner's bony fingers and bounces. With a yelp, the hand disappears, the wooden hatch thuds shut and all goes silent again.

I recover my composure first, feeling all around the entrance for damage. My fingers close around a shred of something. I don't know what it is, but I pocket it anyway, just in case it can be used as evidence against us.

But then there are steps in the distance. Voices.

'Run! Godfrey, run, run!'

I speed out through the doorway, press myself into the shadows across the courtyard and sweep along the stone walls, back up into the small chamber above the kitchen where my father and I dwell.

Fa snores lightly and once more, I praise Heaven for a father who works so hard and sleeps soundly. Godfrey, by the sound of it, was not so lucky. I pray fervently as I hear the struggle outside: guards apprehending a boy much too young to know how to keep his mouth shut.

'I was only exploring. Yes, I know it's the middle of the night! I couldn't sleep and so I decided to walk around. If I am to be a Knight after all, I must train myself not to be afraid. Let go of me! The Lord Maxwell wouldn't want his new Page boy treated thus, would he? Let go of me!'

The low, rumbling voices of the guards grow fainter as they choose what to do with him.

God in Heaven, please do not let him fall into the hands of De Berclay, I pray. If I hadn't meddled, we wouldn't be in this mess.

Forgive, forgive, I truly repent. Godfrey stood up for me and distracted the Commander. Thanks to my own indiscretion, he also knows of the deception, whatever it is.

Does De Berclay sense it?

My only comfort is that the boy is from a noble family, not just a servant as I am. If something happened to Godfrey, there would be questions asked.

Wouldn't there?

READING WIELDS POWER

The next morning there is much to do—men and carts are deployed to the burgh to stock up in earnest, in case the King's army comes our way. Again and again, the terrible stories are told of Berwick, on the opposite coast, where defiance and courage were rewarded with fire and blood only a few short years ago.

Godfrey still keeps to his chamber. I catch sight of him at the window, his eyes reddened, by distress or lack of sleep I cannot tell. I must talk to him. But how?

I can't believe my luck when Fa takes me aside.

'You know the new Page? He is of an ill humour today,' the Lady Maxwell says. She wants him to be treated kindly, so I've made up my mind to send him some fresh bannocks and butter, and the new jam I was keeping for the Yule Feast. If that doesn't cheer his soul, then I know not what will.'

I lower my eyes. 'Would you like me to take it to him?'

'The very thing, Ada. Let me describe where he resides.'

I wait patiently for my father to explain what I already know so well. This is a gift—I need to speak with the boy, and fast. Before De Berclay can do more harm.

'I'm not surprised really,' Fa rumbles on. 'They sever the Page boys from their parents so early. No wonder it's all too much. He'll be fine, so he will, for the Lord Maxwell is one of the kindest noblemen of these lands.'

'But yet he holds that young man in the tower for months.'

I bite my lip. My spirit really is too wild sometimes. Questioning our Lord Maxwell's integrity? Now that would give De Berclay a reason to finish the job he started last night. Thankfully, Fa doesn't question me.

'Lord Maxwell knows best, Ada. Don't doubt your betters. The sooner you learn that lesson, the better. That lad in the tower must be a truly devilish danger to us; that's all there is to it.'

If only he knew. I wipe my hands on my apron and feel it—in the pocket, there is a resistance. Not much, but a little.

Of course—I picked something up by the pit prison.

'What's the matter, Ada?' Fa has placed his hands on his hips and stares at me. I wipe a strand of hair from my face, tuck it back into my braid and lift the tray. 'Nothing. Nothing. Just daydreaming, probably. Pardon, Fa.'

He nods, satisfied, but his eyes still follow me out through the door, up the stairs of the Gatehouse, around the narrow wind and to the door behind which, I am told, Godfrey is resting.

Since my hands are full, I have no choice but to kick the door by want of a knock.

There is nothing but a groan from inside and I shudder. What could the men have done to him last night?

I kick again. 'Your meal, Master Godfrey! It's Ada, the kitchen maid. I have brought some—'

But I don't need to complete my sentence. The door creaks open, and a remarkably well-looking Godfrey helps himself to buttered bannocks as I walk through the door. Crumbs rain from his mouth. He beams. 'About time, Ada. Weren't you wondering what happened?'

'Yes, I was,' I answer, still baffled. 'In fact, I worried all night. Aren't you unwell? I heard you were out of humour.'

His cheeks puff out with food. 'Depends who I'm talking to. The castle guards and Squires came earlier, and I could barely speak. You are here and I am recovered. Isn't it fortunate?' He smiles broadly before the corners of his mouth drop. 'Was the prisoner trying to escape last night, do you think?'

I shrug, self-consciously smoothing my apron— Godfrey's room is so much more decadently furnished than the chamber I share with Fa. 'I can't imagine so. Even if a single hand found purchase on the rim, he could never haul his whole body through. Unless…'

'Unless he had help?' Godfrey completes my sentence. 'But why would we help him escape from the pit of our own castle? If he is locked up in Caerlaverock, there must be a good reason.' He chews thoughtfully.

'Maybe he doesn't know what that reason is,' I muse and Godfrey shrugs. 'So, what did happen to you last night, Godfrey?'

He grins again. 'They wanted to know what I was doing in the tower, as well they might. You probably heard my excuses. De Berclay had his man fetch a whip, and I was truly vexed for a moment, until the guards pointed out that the Lord Maxwell was in charge of my guidance, and that he may not be pleased if I was harmed. My father is a good friend of the family, and our forebears have jointly travelled to the Holy Land. Anyway, much warning, much protesting, much contrition. No harm done.'

My throat is dry. 'Don't underestimate De Berclay, Godfrey. It's too late for me, but you may yet avoid making an enemy of him.' As I speak, I am wringing my hands in my apron pockets, and that's when I feel it again.

'Ada, you look like you have seen a ghost!'

I produce a crumbling piece of cloth from my pocket,

stiff with dirt. My voice catches. I comprehend it as I say it. 'The prisoner. He must have… it's a message!'

We hold it by the window. 'I found this last night, by the trapdoor. I thought it might have come from my own torn garment, but…'

'But it belongs to the prisoner, does it not? Colban Graham.'

'It must.'

We both scrutinise the rag. There are letters, scratched into the muddy fabric, perhaps with a sharp stone. It must have taken some effort to have achieved this in that murky cell.

'Can you make out what it says, Ada?'

I look at him, baffled. 'Godfrey, I'm a laundress—I can't read!'

'Well, I'm only eight. My reading is not very accomplished.'

We stare each other out and it only takes a few seconds for the giggles to claim us both, however serious the situation.

'Bad reading is better than no reading. Go on, Godfrey! Impress me.' I spread the shred of cloth out as best as I can where the light is brightest and wait. I wish I could interpret the scratches on it, forming patterns and lines.

Godfrey wrinkles his nose and narrows his eyes. He cocks his head to the side and licks his lips in concentration. He inclines his head the other way and chews his lip.

And then his eyes widen.

NOT MUCH OF A PLAN

I still don't understand, even as I fetch parchment and quill so that Godfrey may transcribe the message as best as he can. 'So, De Berclay is taking the ransom money and he keeps asking for more, despite such a sum already being paid? And he's doing this in the name of Lord Maxwell—using his seal—without the Lord's knowledge?'

'You are quick, Ada. Yes.'

'Read the message again.'

Godfrey sighs. 'It's nothing but a mud-stained cloth. It was dark. Of course it is a curt message!'

'Read it aloud, Godfrey, I prithee.'

He smooths out the fabric and begins. 'Ransom paid thrice. Commander taking silver for himself. Means to kill me.'

'What if it's a trick? What if he only wants our help? To escape?'

'Ada, can't you see? The messages are going through the Toll Master at Dumfries. You said so yourself, it's underhand. Deceptive. Now we know why.'

Sweat forms in the small of my back. Shivers run all the way up my spine. *Bringing food to a weak prisoner is one thing. Setting him free is quite another.*

'Godfrey, that Squire fought against our own men at Lochmaben; that's where he was captured. He's from over the border. His army killed Commander Robert Cunningham. You never met that man, but he was a real Knight, brave and true.' I'm clutching at straws now and Godfrey knows it.

He squares up to me, holding up his transcription.

'I told you, I can't read it,' I exclaim in frustration.

'Whatever you say, Ada, do you believe De Berclay capable of plotting to kill a defenceless and weakened Squire in the pit? Think: I may be just such a Squire, a few years into the future.'

I sigh. 'I believe that man capable of anything. Yes, even that.'

'Then what is your Christian duty?'

It occurs to me how silly the whole thing is. I'm no Knight. I'm not even a Lady. I don't have the luxury of doing the right thing. My job is to survive, and to keep my head down. 'If De Berclay wanted to kill Squire Graham, he'd have done so by now,' I offer weakly.

'Not if there is more money to be made. Didn't you

take the letter to the Toll Master only days ago? He'll have to prove the prisoner is alive before the family will give more.'

'All right. I admit it's possible. But even if all you say is true, what can we do?'

'We do what is right. Am I not training to be chivalrous? We have to set Colban Graham free.'

I feel a muddy wave of nausea rise in my throat. 'You say it like it's the easiest thing in the world, Godfrey. He may be in danger now, but if we are caught, he will be killed for certain, and the two of us along with him.'

I sweep out through the doorway and back down to the kitchen. Fa raises an eyebrow when I storm through the room and begin peeling turnips with savage vigour. But he chooses to say nothing, which is just as well.

I avoid Godfrey for the next day, and the day after, too. Every time he rides after the men on the pony he has been furnished with, he glances aside, trying to catch my eye, but I do not allow it.

I avoid everybody else, too, truth be told, taking particular care to know where De Berclay is at any given moment, and placing myself at the exact opposite end of the castle to him. So far, it seems to be working. Every time my steps lead me near the Murdoch Tower, I pinch my nose against the stench of impending death. My conscience is like a harp, strung too tight and out of tune. Every time I stare into the distance, across the water where this man's family may make their home, there is a tug, and remorse reels around my mind for hours to come. The castle is an anthill of activity. Supplies are carried hither and thither; riders arrive and depart. Thankfully for me, De Berclay is otherwise occupied. I wonder—if I carried a hunk of bread and a roast pig on my head and danced along the battlements to the tower to feed the prisoner, would anyone notice?

The drawbridge has been lowered to allow supplies into the castle, but just before the gates are closed before sundown, a small cart, pulled by a donkey, appears inside the courtyard. To my surprise, 'tis the very man who took my confession.

'Friar Malcolm from Greyfriars. The Lord Maxwell sent for him to instruct the Lady Maxwell in matters of religion while the Lord Maxwell is away,' says Mary self-importantly as she carries an armful of dirty sheets past me to the wash-house. I stumble after her with a basket of soiled shirts, looking back over my shoulder. The Friar is smaller and rounder than he looked in the kirk, and he is clutching a knapsack, a pile of books and his small Maltese lapdog to his chest.

Fa acknowledges him from the kitchen doorway with a raised hand and strokes his beard.

'I see,' I mumble.

The Friar stumbles on the cobbles as he is led to his Gatehouse chambers below the family quarters.

That night, I find it hard to sleep, especially with the window directly beside my bed. Peeking around the heavy cloth covering, I fancy I see a Godfrey-shaped shadow streak across the courtyard to the tower. I am startled, shamed—but not surprised. I am older, but he is braver. I still have my father, but he has no one here. Some of the castle guards talk to him for sport, but he has every reason to be lonely, and yet…

The moon stands high in the sky, and it is unseasonably warm, even for July. My hair sticks to my face like tar, and whichever way I twist my body on the mattress, a blade of straw jabs my skin, like a prod to my conscience.

I sigh. Wrapping my night clothes tightly around me, and draping a black shawl from Fa's hook over it all for disguise, I follow my friend into the night.

There is a dim light from the Lady Maxwell's window, even this late. She is most likely praying for her husband and his party who have still not returned.

I sneak along silently, and I do well, for Godfrey jumps so hard that he nearly falls down the open trapdoor himself.

'Ada! You could have killed me, sneaking up like this.'

'Hush your voice. Wheesht!'

We listen. Sea. Owls. The rattling of the portcullis chain in the wind. The breeze creeping through the cracks in the stones.

Nothing else, I think. I exhale and lower myself onto

my knees. Peering into the dungeon below, I wait for my eyes to adjust, and there he is. Stained clothes, even in the shadows I can make out that. His blond hair is matted and long, and there is a beard, thin with youth, but a beard all the same.

Godfrey sinks back down beside the opening. 'So, Ada, since you've come to join us, let me catch you up on our plan.'

'Our plan?'

'Yes. To get this prisoner out.'

A voice croaks from the murky pit below. 'Colban Graham. At your service.'

I am simply not used to men declaring themselves 'at my service'; I am usually at their service, carrying platters. It's almost comical that this Knight should observe common pleasantries even in his predicament.

'Very well, do tell me of your plan.'

'There isn't one yet,' Godfrey declares, not blinking once. 'We were just beginning to work on it. But now that there are two of us to help, we may be able to consider new options.'

'I haven't said I'll help yet!' I protest.

'But you are here. You're with us now, whatever misgivings would hold you back.'

There is a sort of logic to what he is saying, in a childish and ridiculous way.

'Sir Colban, can you hear me?' I whisper down.

'Yes. There isn't much time. My kin will soon believe me dead if they don't already. My father will refuse to pay ransom indefinitely—he is shrewd. He will set out for revenge, but with no more gold coming in, the Commander will see no reason to keep me alive before long. He said so himself, and I believe him. I know I am asking a lot of you, young friends, but unless you help me out of here, I shall certainly meet my death in this very hole.'

'Could we throw down a rope?' I offer.

There is a brief hesitation from the man in the pit. 'Maybe, but how would I go about leaving the castle? The bridges will be drawn, and there will be a call of high alert.'

'We need you to leave the castle in broad daylight, across the drawbridge. It's the only way. We will need a disguise,' Godfrey adds.

Now, that makes more sense.

'As a serf, you mean?'

'No, because everybody knows the servants. Perhaps a travelling minstrel? Or a monk? Can you sing—or pray?'

The silence from the pit is deafening.

'What about a seller?' I suggest. We could get a cart onto the castle. Loaded with… with *something*, and you could sell it and leave again with it?'

Godfrey is nodding, and down in the pit, the prisoner

is mumbling. 'That could work. It could! But how long will you need to get it done?'

My mind has gone blank. *Where would I get a cart from unless I steal the Friar's?* It's easier for me than for eight-year-old Godfrey, but it's still pretty much impossible. 'Days. Maybe three…'

There is a groan from the pit. I understand; he wants out of there *now*, and he can't wait until I have got time to devote to his cause.

'It's not much of a plan,' Godfrey observes.

'But it's the only plan we've got, so let's—'

I am interrupted by shouts, many of them. Godfrey and I look at the open trapdoor in alarm and rush forward to shut it which results in an undignified tangle. Panicking, we rush from the tower, but we needn't have worried. People are running from every doorway and corner, even though the sun is barely risen. Candles, torches, clanging and calling. It's hard to make out exactly what, but some sentences are repeated among the din, again and again.

'They're here!'

'The English army is coming over yon hill.'

'They are outside the castle walls.'

'Make safe! Make safe! Make Caerlaverock safe!'

Cold morning air creeps under my clothes and chills me to the bone.

And Godfrey? Godfrey is nowhere to be seen.

THE KING'S ARMY

'Why didn't you waken me when you heard the shouting?'
Fa looks irate, but relieved to see me too.

'I didn't—'

'Never mind that now, girl. What needs to be done?
What needs to be done?'

For a second, I'm misled, thinking that he has
addressed this to me, but of course that can't be the
case—he would never seek my counsel. It unsettles
me deeply, seeing my father flounder like a newborn. I
reach for his hand, but he talks on regardless, to no one
in particular. 'The battlements! They are going to parley
first, aren't they? They will give us the opportunity to
surrender.'

A stone-weight sinks low into my stomach. 'The Lord
Maxwell and his best men are still away from home!'

Fa's look confirms that he has had the same
thought already. We both shudder. But our hesitation

is only momentary. Like every living soul in Castle Caerlaverock, we hurry up a stair or other to see over the battlements, despite the curt instructions to the contrary from the guards. Thankfully, De Berclay is based in the Gatehouse and will not likely come to this part of the castle. The early breeze makes our clothes flutter. Even through the wisps of my hair, I can see a number of ships in the distance on the smooth surface of the Solway Firth. They might be nothing to do with the army at all. Or they might be everything to do with the army. I crane my neck to see and swallow hard. There are so many! Riders upon riders, and over the next few minutes, foot-soldiers flood over the hill and down towards our castle. We remain rooted to the spot.

'Will this procession ever end?' remarks Mary drily. She knows, as we all do, the price of defiance is death. What option can there be for us but to surrender?

My thoughts turn to the prisoner. *Who knows, perhaps Colban Graham's kin are with the King. He may yet walk free if he doesn't suffer damage in the fight.*

But there won't be a fight, will there?

Surely no one in their right mind could choose a fight.

I was young then, but I know that the last Lord Maxwell, Sir Herbert, signed fealty to the English King a few years ago. But after Sir Herbert's death, the clan supported Wallace in his rebellion. That's why these soldiers have come, I realise. Punishment. Lordship. Stamping out the

revolt once and for all, and to capture Wallace while they
are at it, no doubt. He's not hiding here, that's for sure, but
King Edward probably doesn't know that.

'Is Commander De Berclay the one to decide?' I
whisper to Fa. I know he doesn't hold the Commander
in high regard, and there is worry etched around his
eyes. In the clear morning light, he looks older, greyer
than he does in the kitchen. More defenceless.

'De Berclay may recommend a course of action, but
in the Lord's absence, I believe 'tis the Lady Maxwell
who decrees how to proceed.'

Still they come oozing over the hill with their painted
shields, bright flags, tall standards, lances and horses
bearing banners and ribbons. They haven't sent anyone
to parley or negotiate. Instead, in the distance, Knights
try out their steeds, Squires and archers erect colourful
tents, well out of range of our small catapult. It is as if
a city of menace has made camp outside Caerlaverock,
going about their business without a care, while we
inside look on with growing unease.

'We must surrender, for the love of God,' mutters
Mary, standing beside the Lady Maxwell's chambermaid.

At this point, the guards receive a signal from the
top of the Gatehouse Tower and order us back down the
stairs. 'Away with you, away. Orders from Commander
De Berclay. An attack could be imminent! Away, and
ready yourselves as best as you can.' Stragglers at the top

are helped along by ramming shields, and reluctantly, we file back into the courtyard, cursing those who drove us down. Fa and the armoury serf begin to whisper in hushed tones, but I raise my head to see. The Lady Maxwell is standing high on the tower of the Gatehouse, beside De Berclay, Old Walter Weir and two of their Knights. They are talking animatedly; I can see that even from here. On second thoughts, I think De Berclay is urging the Lady to come away, as she must be nearly within firing range of some of their arrow-men. Eventually, she retires back down into her Gatehouse chambers. From there, she must have an excellent view of our shifting sea of enemies, rising like a terrifying tide.

View...

Which reminds me.

I make a run for the small chamber above the portcullis; it has a narrow arrow slot facing out over the north side of the castle, the direction from which the enemy is bound to attack unless we yield before missiles are fired. The chamber is usually occupied by a guard, but I have guessed correctly—they are all out on the battlements, every last one of them, to give the appearance of a true stronghold, well-defended and sufficiently staffed to drive off the army of England itself.

With not more than sixty men here at this time, it's a deception that is unlikely to work.

We try, but I wager that none of us in Caerlaverock

can concentrate on any ordinary task, apart from sneaking glances over the walls whenever we can. The King of England is setting up his court outside! In the distance, we hear harp music and singing, drums and tambourines. Furthest from us on the hill, we see the King's standard emblazoned on a large tent, with as many as five chargers tied up outside it. The sun frames the horses in a golden light, like an invincible heavenly army. I blink.

'Make room for me!' I hear beside me. 'Tis a whisper tinged with worry. Godfrey wriggles to crouch on the floor, peering out through the lower part of the arrow slit while I stand on tiptoes to peer through the top.

We both gasp when in the distance, a single rider in chainmail and metal-breastplate separates out from the densely packed tents and the writhing movement of footmen and archers. Slowly, his handsome black charger trots towards our outer moat.

He must have been chosen for his voice, for it reverberates and bounces off our stone walls like a cannonball: 'Lower the drawbridge and relinquish your castle to the King of these Isles: His Majesty King Edward. Long live the King!' His last cry is echoed by thousands around him.

'Tis harder to make out our soldiers' reply among the din, and our chamber is lower than the battlements, but I clearly discern De Berclay's speech. He will surely have other things on his mind than a meddling laundry maid, but a shiver runs down my spine all the same. The courtyard, on the other hand, is entirely silent. Every castle dweller strains his ears to hear. No wonder. All our lives may depend on this exchange.

Suddenly, I sense movement in the air, just above our window in the archer's chamber and a singing in the wind until there is a thud, a painful scream and a collective roar from the assembled enemies. 'He has been hit! Their messenger has been hit!' Godfrey hisses.

The rider sways in his saddle and, listing badly, awkwardly turns his horse. The beast knows what to do instinctively and trots back the way it came.

But it takes a moment to process what we have just seen.

Did we just shoot the messenger?

'Duck!' yells Godfrey and throws his full weight against me to knock me aside.

Three enemy arrows have found the slit and now lie harmlessly on the stone floor.

Outside, heavy drums begin to pound.

10

IT BEGINS

Every candle in the room flickers to the beat of our destruction.

We stare at each other and understand.

There will certainly be a siege now, and an attack. The best soldiers the King of England has at his disposal, more than 3000 of them, against just over sixty in our castle.

And there is nothing we can do about it.

I give a small shriek as my garments are pulled from behind.

'Ada! You are wanted this minute. We must ration food and decide what will keep and what will not. We must make preparations, and the Lady Maxwell will still want her breakfast.' Fa sounds energetic and certain again, only his words pour out faster and a little shriller than normal. He hardly seems to notice that Godfrey is in the room too.

But Godfrey is no serf. He will be at his leisure to remain here, watching events unfold.

My feet hurt as Fa drags me along the rough steps and back to the kitchen. I know he means well, but his nervousness bleeds out through every pore of his reddened face. His voice, normally low and gentle, has a knife-edge to it now.

Churning butter at speed is not how you're meant to do it. It's a thing you do when you sit in the corner of the kitchen by the fire, while humming a song, or listening to a bard who has come down from the Great Hall for a bite to eat. 'Tis a thing you do while you chat about comings and goings, by fading light as the night draws in. But Mary and I sit in the kitchen, churning and churning as the cream will not keep otherwise. Fa has given both of us a handful of salt to add, to prolong the life of the food.

Mary is more quarrelsome than ever, glaring out of the narrow doorway.

'If there is fighting, there will be deaths. If we lose, what will become of us then? At best, we will be turned out of the castle.'

I shrug, but I don't think it matters whether I respond or not. Her voice rises by an octave.

'Scotland has leaders. Where are *they* when we need them, tell me that! Here is an army sent to bring about our ruin and who will defend us? Wallace? Balliol? Think of it, the Lord Maxwell is still away from home, abandoning us all in our time of need!' She wipes her nose and scratches her chin, a sure sign that proper tears are not far away. Fast steps pass us in the courtyard every few seconds. The horses whinny and voices shout. *Spin, spin, spin the handle on the churner, Ada.* Its predictable rhythm soothes me: it's something I can do.

It's hard to imagine that outside, arrows continue to fly. Out there beyond Caerlaverock's thick walls, a mere stone's throw from where I am sitting, chargers gallop with Knights on their backs, tents and banners and flags flutter in the breeze and, for all I know, King Edward himself is taking his dinner. It's happening, but at the same time it isn't. It doesn't feel real.

I'm startled by Mary resuming her lament. 'I know what they'll do,' she sobs. 'They'll send the few fighting men they have to stand on the battlements where they'll be hit and where they'll die. DIE!' Mary almost screams it, and finally, Fa cracks.

'MARY! ENOUGH! That will do. Now, wheesht, the two of you while I work out what we need to do next.'

Thankfully, my butter is finally churned, and I shake out my arm which has gone numb.

'Don't be idle, Ada! Shape the butter into rounds and wrap them, will you. Then head to the cold-store and lower them in there but be sure to choose a barrel that closes properly. Now of all times, we can't afford the mice and rats to get our food. Who knows how long before this army loses interest?'

He strides away, tucking a strand of his greying hair behind his ears and shooing the cat away from the fire and into the larder at this talk of mice.

I exhale, shake my arm out one last time and rise to look for empty barrels in the scullery. I stack the butter carefully and close the lid. *To the cold-store now.* Staggering down the stairs with my load, I nearly trip over the final step and stop. The courtyard is strewn with missiles, chiefly stones and rocks. There are men on the battlements, and several are gathering up the scattered ammunition, keeping a watchful eye on the sky for fear there should be more deadly rain.

'Move!' shouts one of the young guards and I press myself into a gap, still holding the barrel.

'Wherever you're going, do so quickly, and stay inside after that.' The exasperation in his voice is badly concealed. 'Look, that stupid maid just decides to cross the courtyard,' he shouts over his shoulder. His colleague shakes his head at me too.

'I've been *sent* to the cold-store.'

I sprint across towards the Murdoch Tower. It may not be the exact location of the cold-store, but it is only a little out of my way. The prisoner must be terrified. It would be cruel to leave him ignorant of our plight.

I place my barrel on the ground and carefully lift the trapdoor.

'Squire Graham! It's Ada. The castle is under attack.'

There is a reverberating sort of echo down here. As if somehow, the walking of six thousand feet and the sound of three thousand voices could creep into the very foundation of the building and roar through the walls.

'Who?' The voice sounds weaker than before. Mind you, anyone would lose the force of life down here.

'The English army. The King himself is leading them.'

'How many?' It is barely a croak.

'Over three thousand, I'm told. I've got to go.'

'Ada, wait!'

He says that too loudly and I slam the hatch down in a panic, dragging my barrel along the ground after me. To the cold-store now, and no delay.

But delay is exactly what fate has in mind.

As soon as I reach the courtyard, there is a crash, a noise so deafening that it must surely be reserved for the most terrifying part of Hell. I can't help it, the barrel simply glides from my hand, smashes onto the ground and rolls sideways towards the horses. Some of them have risen onto their hind legs, slamming their hooves down on air and stone, or kicking out from behind. Only now do I become aware of whinnying and of the panicked shouts of men.

Old Sir Walter Weir, De Berclay's second in command, lies on the ground, his breastplate badly dented and an arrow in his left shoulder where his chainmail is torn.

Oh Lord, what do I do? I bend down to open the visor on his helmet and force myself to look at his pain-twisted face. I know him as such a kind man, with a twinkle in his eye and authority in his voice. But not now. Now he lies bleeding and clutching his chest. The worst bit is that none of his men are able to tend to him.

They are up on the battlements hurling stones and screaming, although some of their voices are hoarse already. De Berclay stomps past, casts a look at the injured Sir Walter and says nothing. Staring straight ahead, he marches back to the Gatehouse Tower and disappears.

Another crash rents the air and the terrifying sound of crumbling masonry is drowned out by cheers from outside the castle walls. Soon, the enemies' voices unite in an organised chant. Helplessly, I look at the man at my feet, and try to work out what on earth to do next. There is a shriek of distress behind me. It's Godfrey! He joins me at Old Sir Walter Weir's side and kneels. A rock the size of five men's fists slams onto the ground not two paces away from us.

All the colour has drained from Godfrey's freckled face. 'We must get him to safety, Ada. There is only us.'

I nod and attempt to hook my elbows beneath the old Knight's arms. He is a tall man and unwieldy. Two children could barely carry his armour, never mind the man with it. I stagger, despite not having moved him a single ell. 'Help us!' I shout up to the soldiers on the battlements, but they are engaged in battle and oblivious to our plight. At my feet, the old man goes floppy with pain, his eyes rolling to reveal the white.

11

OLD SIR WALTER WEIR

Godfrey looks panicked now, glancing up at the sky and flinching at every whistle in the air. He is right to. Enemy crossbows reach far, and some find their targets as if guided by an invisible force.

'Sir Walter needs shelter,' I groan to Godfrey and pull as hard as I can, but the heavy man is almost not shifting at all. 'Push, Godfrey!' I snap.

'I am! With all my strength!' Despite the danger, outrage sparks from his eyes. His short body slouches like a wounded dog.

I flinch as another arrow lands a few feet from me and bounces on the cobbles. A cry from above: one of our guards must have struck down an enemy. There is a small moment of backslapping and then the fight continues.

'My father will know how to move Sir Walter,' I shout and run to the kitchen door, but neither Fa nor Mary are there.

What now?

'Hurry, Ada!' Godfrey is cradling the injured man's head. Old Sir Walter has opened his eyes, but his teeth are bared in pain and although he doesn't shout, there is an animal-like guttural groan which is harder to bear than anything else. I look around. *What other option do we have?*

A thought forms, like a wisp of smoke, barely there. It thickens like steam until it fills my mind with its rebellious mist.

'Stay with him, Godfrey. I'll fetch help.'

'Help from where?' he moans, but I'm already speeding along the cobbles, ducking missiles.

'Hurry, Ada.' I hear him shout behind me.

I don't know what possesses me, but every thought of propriety, loyalty or decency has simply evaporated. With a bit of luck, and if I am exceedingly courageous, I might be able to right two wrongs today.

There is dust. Shouting. Whizzing of objects as they slice through the air above our heads. The smell of smoke, too, as flaming missiles find dry wood.

In the distance, De Berclay supervises a large vat being hoisted up to the top of the Gatehouse Tower. They must expect a breach soon, or else they would not be wasting precious oil. I can see the steam from here and wince in pity for our opponents, however outnumbered and threatened we are.

Man tormenting man. There is no glory in it.

I'm nearly there, squeezing past the shying animals, patting necks and stroking manes in exchange for easy passage. There—a ladder, leaning against the inside wall of the Murdoch Tower, as if to say '*Go on, laundress. Help yourself.*'

I do, kicking the trapdoor open to a startled cry from below. No pretence of secrecy now. Quite the contrary— it feels like there is someone else in my shoes now, not Ada at all, but someone strong and defiant, a warrior who takes a risk—and lives or dies by it.

I drag the ladder towards the opening, but I'm knocked off my feet by something heavy and hard hitting the wall outside. The dust settles. I don't have the luxury to discuss what I'm doing—time for that later. Maybe. The sun is slowly going down and we are vulnerable, all of us. *Thud, thud, thud* go the missiles, most likely rocks from their catapults hitting our wooden structures. Horses whinny; distant screams mingle with the cawing of the crows. I hear pounding hooves and again and again, the whistle of weaponry, the rush of rocks, ripping through the air.

With a scrape, the ladder lands at the prisoner's feet.

'What are you going to do to me?' the Squire demands, his voice shakier than he probably wants it to sound.

I poke my head into the opening. 'It's only me, Ada. I need your help now. I imagine that, before long, you'll need mine. It seems a fair barter. Don't tarry.'

I don't know why I say that last bit because he bounds up the wobbly ladder like a field mouse, in long, jumping strides.

'Come and help me. Trust me,' I demand and together, we pull the ladder back up and lean it into the same place where it stood before. I bend down and close the trapdoor with a heavy clank and slide the bar back across it.

He narrows his eyes at me with suspicion. 'Why?'

I turn away because, honestly, I don't know the answer myself. Dragging him by his sleeve, I pull him out into the courtyard where dusk is gathering. Flames fly above, but less often now. On the battlements, I can see the guards lighting some sort of missile, no more than rags, tied together with rope and soaked in something flammable.

'Ada! Be quick.' Godfrey is still crouched by the motionless body of the old man and doesn't even look up, although the stench alone should alert him to the prisoner. 'All together,' I command and with remarkable strength for one held captive so long, Colban Graham makes the impossible possible. Men run past us with leather slings, gathering the rocks in the courtyard to throw them down on the enemy again, hollering and shouting. The sun is about to disappear below the horizon for good tonight, but it sends a farewell ray and the prisoner's head is suddenly illuminated like a principal image in a manuscript. Godfrey gasps.

'I had no choice, Godfrey. We needed help and this one was the only man I could think of who wasn't occupied.' With my free hand, I grab Godfrey's hat and press it down on Squire Graham's head. 'The proper disguise must come later. We need to get Sir Walter out of harm's way first.'

We have become all but invisible. No one pays the prisoner the smallest heed. Godfrey's mouth, however, still hangs open in the shape of a dead fish. At least he comes willingly, with me leading the way to the kitchen.

The candles on the sconces are alight and I quickly throw a handful of branches on the range where the smouldering flames are quick to dance, casting shadows onto the walls. I bend down to reach for a goblet and a jug of wine. 'Gently does it,' hushes Godfrey, even though he can't possibly have any idea of what to do for the best. It feels as if my heart is beating at thrice the speed of normal. The injured man stirs, but his breaths are heavy and hard.

'His chainmail and armour,' Colban Graham mutters urgently. 'We must remove it all. Look at that dent! It's cutting into his ribs.' He gestures and I see it too—and turn my face away almost immediately.

My hands tremble. I have never disarmed a man before—the clasps and buckles and straps confound my senses and make me sweat even more profusely than I was before. I stare helplessly. Godfrey shakily rattles the fixings.

'I don't know where to begin.'

The prisoner looks down on the man. Most likely, the injured Sir Walter was involved in his capture. Maybe it was *he* who tied the rope around the Squire's wrists, maybe it was *he* who pushed him into the gloomy dungeon of the Murdoch Tower—although I cannot believe that he would have delighted in it.

A humming noise begins. Gentle, quiet. Pious even. 'I can't do it without this—it aids my memory.'

Slowly and methodically, the ragged prisoner undoes the clasps, unknots the straps, slides and unlocks the layers of metal, humming as the iron layers scrape apart and the chainmail rattles. The injured Sir Walter inhales more deeply, calmed by the strange music. Still the young man hums while Godfrey and I look on.

'I am a Squire. What do you expect? Of course I know about armour,' he says, while his hands keep moving and he resumes his odd melody. Part by part, the armour-plates are set aside, the heavy helmet last of all, to reveal a couple of bloody weals.

Godfrey swallows hard. 'Is he going to die?'

He has said what we must all be thinking.

The soul is attached to the body but by a thread which can sever at any moment...

I rush to the range and set a bucket of water above the fire. 'Fa says that cleaning a wound is halfway to healing.' I hesitate. 'But we'd better send for the Friar, just in case.'

There is a commotion outside, sudden and loud—angry voices and a flash of light. Squire Graham starts. Of course, if he is discovered now, there will be no mercy at all. The few fighting men we have inside are needed to battle the thousands outside the castle. No one can be spared to guard a prisoner. I whirl round as Fa hastens in, holding a pail and dropping a handful of pewter dishes.

'The hay for the horses has been hit. Quickly, before the fire spreads, hurry! Where's Mary?' he snaps without looking at me. I glance sideways but Colban Graham has melted away into a shady corner of our kitchen, a small piece of his torn tabard showing behind the sacks of flour. I can only hope my father doesn't notice the smell of one who hasn't washed or used a latrine for months.

Fa absorbs the wounds of the old Knight laid out on the table and gives a low whistle, but he doesn't slow down.

'What are you two staring at? Run and help! We'll need to see to the wounded later. For now, let's make sure we don't all burn alive betwixt these walls!' He snatches the water from the range and stomps out with it. I fancy I hear a relieved exhale from behind the flour sacks.

'Now!' Fa shouts from outside.

'Come on, Godfrey!'

Reluctantly, the Page follows me into the smoky courtyard and I wonder whether we are abandoning two men to their deaths in that kitchen. How can the prisoner possibly escape undetected, weak as he is?

My heart falls into even deeper despair when I see De Berclay march purposefully towards the southern end of the castle, his henchman at his side.

COVETING

Mercifully, I have little time to dwell on De Berclay, Colban Graham or even Fa—the flames puff themselves up like proud peacocks into the night sky, trying to strike fear into our very fibre. We pass pails of water along from the castle well. From a distance, the horses witness their feed consumed by crackles and sparks. Pounding the cobbles and flaring their nostrils, they shy back from the open courtyard where objects and rocks are still landing—albeit less frequently.

I glance up into the dusky sky each time I make the trip to the well, hauling the bucket chain when it's my turn. My father's leather apron is singed and blackened. Exhausted guards have slid down the walls on the battlements, affording themselves a little rest betwixt duties.

We have taken to extinguishing the last of the flames in the hay with saddle blankets. No more hay, for it's all ruined. There is some grain for the horses, but not enough. Not nearly enough. The truth is, we may need the grain ourselves before long.

But these are worries for the next day, or the day after that.

'I will return to my quarters,' Godfrey announces pompously. But I am not so easily fooled. He is a boy, pale and as near to tears as I have seen him. Old Sir Walter Weir has been kind to him.

'You need to sleep, as do all of us.' Fa straightens up and leans against the wall. 'For us, Ada, there is more work to be done. The Lady Maxwell still needs to eat. As do our men.'

Both Fa and I can barely stand. How can Caerlaverock possibly be guarded at night, against such an army which can easily spare and rest hundreds of soldiers at a time?

I find that I am too tired to care.

It is long past suppertime, past Compline even, and the Lady and her companions will surely be at their prayers. We return to the kitchen where the Friar kneels by the injured Sir Walter. The scent of holy oil lingers in the air—the last rites for a dying man. I try not to draw attention to myself, but I can't help moving a little closer. Colban Graham clearly used his time well. The injured Knight's wounds are bandaged skilfully with strips torn from the old man's sleeve and some herbs from the sill in the kitchen, still showing under the dressing. A little flour has been spilled, too. The only other sign that the prisoner was ever here.

My eyebrows shoot up: the chainmail and the bent armour has also vanished. Even after so many months in the darkness, this Squire still has all his wits about him. He has taken the wounded man's armour as a disguise! Where could he be now? And—my gut contracts with guilt—what will he do next? I don't know him, after all. I doubt he would hurt Godfrey or me, and he was kind to Sir Walter, I suppose, but the others—what about them?

Shaking my head to rid myself of fear, I attempt to be of use to Fa. As if no missiles were flying outside, as if no burning arrows were whistling across our roofs, we set to work. Even Mary joins us, fresh from attending to an injured archer.

I mutter the commands aloud to myself, not trusting my over-crowded mind to remember: *Knead the flour and the water into dough. Add the precious salt and a very little sugar from the block. Knead and knead until it yields as my father heats the oven and as the stew bubbles in the pot over the range.*

I drink in the bread-smell, looking for peace when there is none to be found. Crusty and hard, it emerges from the tray and I cut into the steaming loaves, hollow them out and ladle in the stew.

'You may have to carry it in yourself,' Fa mumbles, wiping his hands on his hose.

Of course, the Steward and scullions are helping to guard the battlements overnight to give the men a chance to rest. And so it happens that I carry my tray up the stairs of the Gatehouse into the Great Hall where the Lady Maxwell and her elderly aunt sit in silence by a makeshift altar in the corner, listening and wincing at every whistle of a missile.

They don't seem to see me at all. Feeling my feet crush the rushes and dried lavender on the floor, I straighten up as best as I can, even though this reveals more of the stains on my shift. Lifting my chin in a hopefully dignified manner, I place the platters in front of them.

Close by, I am struck by her beauty. '*The Lady Maxwell eats like a bird,*' Fa has been saying, and I know what he means now. She is a young woman, but childless thus far—although only married for a few months and with her husband away so often, it doesn't necessarily mean that she's cursed. She is thin, this much I can see, and her pale face matches the white faces in the tapestries on the stone walls. After a brief prayer, they begin to eat, but so slowly that the bread-bowls will surely soak through long before they have finished the stew.

I attend to them from the side of the room, standing in the shadows and taking every opportunity to steal a glance out through the arrow slits as the candles burn inside.

With nightfall, there are no further attacks against

the walls, and I am grateful. But even at this hour, every faraway noise from outwith the castle is like a glimpse of Hell to me. We may barely hear them, but there are thousands just yonder, lying in tents, eating their fill, plotting against us. If I strain my ears, I hear the jangle of metal—could they be throwing chains and hooks to climb our walls? There are voices too—could they be planning an assault through the night? I'm sure that was a scraping sound—are they digging beneath the keep? Moreover, there are low calls and horses' hooves and music, yes *even* music—The King must travel with a minstrel, or perhaps several. For a moment, my mouth curls up as I imagine Caerlaverock being the subject of a siege song or some such poem. *Stop Ada! As if we were the stuff of legend!*

But I am most startled by a quiet, close-by sound, so quiet that I almost don't notice it—the voice of the Lady Maxwell speaking to her aunt.

'What can be the hope of my Lord Maxwell returning betwixt now and dawn?'

She has forgotten I am here. Or why would she speak so frankly?

'I fathom, none. Steel yourself, Niece. Your home is strong, and the rocks aren't doing it much damage. We may yet be able to hold out. Is the King of England really going to persist with Caerlaverock when he might take Stirling or Scone? Those would be prizes indeed.

Besides, don't forget that the whole Burgh of Dumfries is even now united in pleading for us before the Almighty. Courage, Niece.'

'Do you believe my Lord Maxwell can persuade the clans to come to our aid, Aunt?'

'I don't know.' The old woman clears her throat briskly. 'All I do know is that we are here and your husband is not; and we have to make the best of it. But I am surprised: De Berclay is missing, you say? If he doesn't return to the Gatehouse soon, you will have to step up and command the men, as the Lady of the Castle. But don't forget, you have the relic from the Holy Land. The protection of the Almighty is surely on this place—you heard the Friar.'

There is a sound, something betwixt a sob and a cough. The knives with which the ladies eat are placed beside the half-hollowed chunks of bread and from my dim vantage point, I can see the older woman's arm gently cradle the shoulder of the younger. The aunt's greying hair shows beneath her wimple as the two women lean into one another.

I forget about the siege, and the Lord Maxwell and the prisoner and imagine what it would have been like to grow up with a mother, or a sister. To have a shoulder of comfort and a face to smile upon you even in the bleakest of hours. I don't want Lady Maxwell's riches, but oh, at this moment I do covet this kind of love with all my heart.

The chairs scrape back, the women rise, take another look through the small window, staying well back from the opening, and walk slowly towards the chamber that houses the makeshift chapel.

I don't know, are they ever concerned with those who clear their tables and cook their food? Do they ever ask themselves who overhears and who might betray?

It is simple. They are the Maxwells; I am nobody.

Sighing, I walk to the table to collect the plates and dishes. I don't need help. Alas, the appetites of the ladies are much less extravagant that those of the Lords.

But then my brain catches up with what I have heard, and I give an involuntary shiver.

De Berclay is missing?

13

THE BELL TOLLS

Despite this being high summer and the hours of darkness short, it feels like the longest of earthly nights. I'm only knee-deep in sleep while Fa's snores and whimpers prove that he is swimming through muddy dreams. I know not which is better.

I pray, certainly, and hope it does some good after my sinful coveting. I pray for the army to be gone by morrow. I pray for Old Sir Walter Weir to recover, and for the Almighty to protect the castle from evil scheming, should Colban Graham have betrayal in mind. For protection from De Berclay I ask, too.

Much keeps me awake. Intermittent shouts from the battlements come as unpredictably as stray arrows, some English Knight or other is always hoping to prove his valour by approaching the castle walls closely. Judging by the calls of the guards, some are wading through the moats in the dead of night, throwing themselves against the gates and the castle walls with great clanging and rattling of their armour. It achieves little for their cause, beyond proof of their courage.

There is something else I can't quite put my finger on—the sea sounds different tonight—closer. The pattern of the waves is broken, I fathom. *Have the clans come to our aid?*

But my speculation comes to an abrupt end as the grey light of dawn edges over the horizon: the bell, that dreaded sound. Where he lies, Fa's eyes crack open. The sound of death; the summoning to Heaven or to Hell. I know for whom the bell tolls. It has to be. Poor Old Sir Walter.

'Come, Ada!' Fa only speaks two words, and yet I know what he asks. We cast our sheets aside and kneel, crossing ourselves to ease Sir Walter's soul's departure from this earth.

The bell has stopped ringing. As if we needed any reminding of our predicament, missiles and rocks start to slice into the castle walls and fly into the courtyard again. There is a chill in my core as I realise, the army outside is cheering. They, too, heard the bell toll and are celebrating this good man's death. Through my tears, I hope his spirit haunts them, whatever happens to us next.

'Ada. We must make ourselves useful.' Fa's hand brushes gently past my cheek. Far from the usual silence of the early morning, the castle courtyard is almost as busy as the burgh on market day. Squires are helping each other into their armour, with many pointing down at the enemy camp to the north. The curtain walls at the western side of the castle look safe enough for now and I climb up to the top to take a look. Nobody pays me any heed which is the way I want it.

But the scene before me takes my breath away.

From here, I can see much of the whole hillside, but the green grass is obscured by the bustle of war. Who would have thought that a warring army could appear more vivid than the brightest tapestry, richer than the feasts and the pageants? The enemies are stirring just as we are, probably more men than I have ever seen in my life. And not ordinary men, no: grand Knights, their coats of arms prominently displayed on their shields, on their tents, on their flags. Well-fed horses graze around our toun's abandoned cottages, their glossy coats shining in the dew. Bowmen and crossbowmen huddle together for warmth, with many of them attending to their equipment. Fires already burn nearby, ready to set their missiles alight.

I fill my lungs with air in an attempt to still my troubled heart.

However hard I try, I cannot fathom how many men there might be. Throwing caution to the wind for a moment, I risk leaning out, intending to stretch and see as far as possible. But instead, a gust of wind forces my hair into my eyes. In shaking it away, I turn my face downwards and my whole body convulses with shock.

God have mercy!

In the shadow of the castle walls, around ten enemy soldiers drag enormous beams of wood along towards their camp on the other side, obscured from view unless our lookouts lean right over as I do now. I follow their trail backwards with my eyes as I try to make sense of this. Concealed by the southern towers, but just visible, there are two ships which must have moored in the shallow waters of the Firth overnight. The sea fog half-hides their movement, but sailors are lowering more huge wooden constructions, like the one I saw carried, into the water and are floating them to land near the southern edge of the moat. Which can only mean one thing.

'Siege engines,' I mutter, as if testing my voice, as well as my strength and my courage. *Everybody's attention is north, on the enemy camp.*

'SIEGE ENGINES,' I shout, forcefully enough to be heard by our guards across the courtyard. Pointing down the side of the castle, I can only repeat my warning in desperation and then the confirmation comes: my call is echoed inside the castle with Gaelic curses.

Missiles and rocks still lie scattered across the flat areas of the battlement from last night, and I barely think, but rush and heave the biggest rock I can lift. Over it goes and lands with a thud beneath, scraping along the stone of the outer wall, resulting in a startled cry. I don't think I hit a man, there would have been a clang of armour. But leaning over *now* would be a mistake, I think.

My judgement is confirmed immediately; two arrows shoot up in the exact space where my head was a second ago. If I manage to throw down more rocks, I may be able to slow the progress of the siege engine to the enemy camp to the north of the castle.

The sound of many footsteps thud on the wooden stairs, with the rattle of loose armour, hurriedly fastened. Seconds later, a squall of Squires bursts onto the battlements, careful to keep their heads down—apart from one who is so small he doesn't have to stoop— Godfrey.

He gives me a quick glance, but among his equals, there is no need to acknowledge a maid. I am oddly grateful: the world, restored to how it ought to be, if only for a moment.

'Out of our way, girl! We need space to move up here.' The leading Squire doesn't know my name, and he doesn't look me in the eye either. Relieved, I duck down onto the stairs once more. Alarm bells, rather than the death knell, are ringing out across the castle now, in unfamiliar rhythms which must serve as signals among the soldiers.

A thin wisp of smoke is rising from the kitchen—Fa is sparing with the wood to save it running out, I imagine. I should go down to help him. The memory of the thick, solid beams of the siege engine swims before my eyes, glistening with Solway water. I cannot help it: my feet carry me right past the kitchen door and towards the armoury where soldiers with bloodshot eyes run in and out to collect weapons, repair arrows and gather pickaxes. In the courtyard, the walls of the outbuildings are being demolished for rocks, blow by blow, with a line of washerwomen, scullions and stable boys standing by to take the newly hewn missiles to the battlements.

They don't notice me as I edge towards the arrow slits for a front-on view. In these lower chambers, I am just across the moats from the besieging army and once again, it strikes icy horror into my heart. The warm summer sun may rise, but there is violence and terror on the earth below it. Out on the northern esplanade, enemy archers are busy assembling the first siege engine.

Of course, I checked carefully when I came in. De Berclay should be directing operations from this very room. Still, no sign of him. Where could he be?

A man of deception and greed he is, skilled in tricking his way into the trust of his betters. But disappear altogether? That is new; unexpected.

And, in my opinion, worthy of investigation.

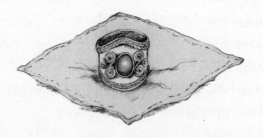

14

THE HOARD

All of our men are now engaged in combat. At one point, I think I spy a bent breastplate on the southern battlement, but it melts away into nothing so quickly in the din that I must have imagined it.

De Berclay is not a man I want to confront, but my curiosity simply gets the better of me. Betwixt facing the enemy and solving a puzzle, I know what I'd sooner do. The Murdoch Tower is all but empty, only guarded at the top by two newly posted sentries who are now keeping an eye for new arrivals by sea. The giant pieces of wood keep coming, despite our desperate attempts to slow them down. The angle is simply too steep to shoot at them. When I am sure that there is no one around, I risk a peek into the pit prison, half expecting De Berclay to be kept safe there, maybe by Squire Graham—but no, there is no sign of life below. I run past many an opening, many a chamber, but the Commander of the castle is nowhere to be seen—is he injured? Dead perhaps? My soul stirs a little at that, however much I despise him. He is not a coward, surely? No coward could be named Commander of a castle such as ours, could they?

I'm about to give up and return to my father's fireside when a terrible thought strikes me. He wouldn't…

Not at a time like this. He wouldn't…

The more I think about it, it is in fact the best opportunity he is ever likely to have. Up in a chamber just above the family's quarters, the Lord Maxwell keeps his hoard: gold and jewels, a terribly valuable ring—and most precious of all, a vase from his father's crusade to the Holy Land. It is said to contain a priceless relic: a bone from St Andrew himself. If De Berclay believes the castle's fall is inevitable, it almost makes sense to steal it, in a twisted, covetous way.

I tiptoe past the brewhouses, up past the Great Hall where the Lady Maxwell and her aunt will likely be watching the progress of the battle, through the hidden gap behind the tapestry, which I help beat free of dust every week, and up a narrow, narrow set of steps, at the end of which is a room with a locked door.

Only it isn't locked at this moment. It hangs slightly ajar, creaking faintly on its broken hinges. The room beyond is dark, though I can smell the recent presence of a candle. Slowly, I step forward, but there is no sound. If I am discovered, I will need a better explanation than mere guesswork, but no one is likely to discover me here anyway.

The casket's lid is open. This is odd. The velvet cloth lies draped over the jewels, as it does when I am here to clean the tapestries, but it looks different today. With trembling fingers, I reach for the cloth and push it aside a little. There is no tinkling of silver, nor the gentle song of pearl against jewel. But there is a rustling. A firmer touch confirms it: beneath the velvet is nothing but jaggy blades of straw.

I gasp, partly from surprise and partly from De Berclay's voice, right in my ear. 'You again!'

I am thrown against the wall and hear a crack in my wrist accompany the dull thud of skin against stone. Winded for a moment, I sink to the ground, but the Commander yanks me upright, holding me by collar of my shift. He leans out through the doorway, assuring himself that no one is coming. *No one is coming.* I cough, earning myself a sharp clip around the back of my head and a hiss.

'Interfering betwixt a man and his providence again! You know too much, maid. That can be forgiven. But I suspect you tell too much too, and that's a risk I cannot take. It would have been better for you not to meddle in the affairs of your betters. But it's too late for you now.'

With this, he pats a clinking purse attached to his belt, sinks his dirty fingernails into my scalp and yanks me down the hidden stair and towards the lower walkway. There, he pulls a deep hood over his face. Above us, we continue to hear shouting and the low thuds of rocks from the outside. De Berclay grins, but it is a heartless grin, borne out of greed, excitement and risk. I don't know why I don't scream, but I just can't. He pushes me down into the lower level of the wine store, with barrels and jugs rattling against one another. In the dim light, I wince back from the shine of metal: he is pointing his sword at me.

If he traps me here, no one will find me. I'll be dead long before anyone investigates, especially with the army outside.

'Good Sir, I do not know what I have done to offend thee.' I begin. Again, he checks the velvet purse on his belt and glances up.

'I am only doing what I must to survive,' De Berclay mutters, perhaps not wholly at ease with his own words. 'This ransom here, for example. Graham can rot in the pit for eternity; I care not. I'll line my purse. But then this! When Caerlaverock falls, the Master will hardly miss a little gold, a little silver—or the odd vase from the Crusades.'

'But the castle is locked down, the bridges are drawn, the portcullis—'

I slow down, comprehension dawning slowly on my foggy brain. 'There is another way out?'

My voice is small, matching the rustling of mice between the stones. Down here, the sounds of battle may as well be sounds of another world. But wait—that sound is not mice at all. Someone is scraping! *Right beneath my feet.*

De Berclay's lips slit to reveal his rotting teeth. He edges backwards and, using his foot, moves an empty crate beside me to reveal a crudely dug hole.

A TUNNEL.

Out pops the head his henchman. 'Brought a visitor, Commander? I thought we'd agreed, no witnesses.'

'There won't be. I'm just passing the time in edifying conversation,' De Berclay leers as he reaches into one of the wine barrels and lifts out a sack of clinking coins, beads, jewels and pearls. Then he uses both hands to pass down a parcel wrapped in velvet cloth. The treasure disappears into the hole. The clinking dulls before being swallowed up by earthen walls. The man is gone.

'You'll be discovered, Commander,' I grunt, more confidently than I feel.

'Touching. But fear not. I'll be gone before anyone can ring a bell.'

'The army outside will discover you then, and will treat you harshly.'

He sniggers. 'Ah, you have spirit, I'll grant you that. But consider it for a moment. I emerge on the outside and offer the King's Knights easy passage into the castle, beneath the moat and into here, where all they have to do is step over the body of a newly slain maid. The King of England will reward me richly, maybe even take me into his own employ to repay my service, and in the meantime, I'll live comfortably on the Lord Maxwell's treasure. The ring alone will fetch enough to buy ten horses, I hear.'

'How can you be so disloyal? God will punish you.'

'The Holy Scriptures say something about being as cunning as foxes, don't they? With the relic from the Holy Land protecting me, I won't come to any harm.'

Does the man's ungodliness know no limit?

He leans towards me. 'It is almost a shame. You might have made some unlucky peasant a meddling wife one day,' he shrugs. 'But now I better take my leave.'

My heart beats fast and it is as if every sense in my body sharpens. It's him—or me.

He steps forward. The sharp blade of his sword reflects the little light and catches his eye—he is looking at my neck. He plans to swing his sword across! Keeping my eyes on his hands, I see his knuckles tense and take my only chance. I duck. The sword slices through the damp air of the storeroom, just where my head was a blink before. His whole heavy body is bearing down on me now and I propel myself forward, guessing rightly that he'll keep his stride wide for balance. At the exact moment that I wriggle through his legs, with the sword's impact sending sparks into the gloom, the door to the room flies open. My lashes moisten with relief: is it a Knight, or a Squire, at least?

But my eyes only travel up to the determined face of an eight-year-old Page.

An eight-year-old Page who has no chance against the experienced warrior. De Berclay knows it, too. He doesn't speak at all, but kicks the door shut with a clang and raises his sword once more—directly over Godfrey's head.

I can't hope to knock a grown man in chainmail off his feet, so it is Godfrey who feels the full force of my body as I throw myself across the room and scream, kicking a flask of wine sideways to distract our assailant.

'HELP US,' I yell at the top of my voice, but the sound merely bounces back at me from the rock and earthen walls. I stretch for the nearest thing I can reach, a small barrel of expensive imported wine. Fa would kill me himself if he knew I was wasting it, but there is no choice. The barrel flies at De Berclay's head. He side-steps just in time and it smashes against the stone. Drenched in the blood-like liquid, he roars towards us, his sword spinning. It's over.

We press our backs against the wall. My hand finds Godfrey's. If I am to die unconfessed at this man's hand, I want company on the way to Purgatory. Although Godfrey is bound to have been guided better for the afterlife.

The silver blade whirls towards us, along with droplets of sweat and spit.

Suddenly, the door crashes open from the outside, with a force I would never have been capable of. It slams into the approaching Commander's face, embedding his sword into the rough-hewn wood. His knees crumple first, his eyes freeze, his arms drop limply by his side. And with a final shake of his mail, he drops to the ground.

Godfrey and I look at each other.

Slowly, we turn our heads towards the open door.

15

BURIED TREASURE

'Tis a man with torn chainmail and a scratched helmet covering his face. The visor is down and obscures his eyes.

'Godfrey, look. Look at the dent in his breastplate!' I whisper.

'Is that the prisoner?' Godfrey asks, trembling.

I nod, transfixed by the tall figure with a broadsword the length of my whole body. I try to speak, but only a toad-like croak comes out.

'I'm glad to have been of service,' the Squire says. 'You have nothing to fear from me.'

I steady myself against the doorway. All the air in the small cellar isn't enough to fill my desperate lungs.

Suddenly, there is a noise, a thud and then a call from the tunnel below: 'Hark, De Berclay! Are you done with that maid yet?'

The tunnel! Colban Graham has understood without

explanation and prises the door to the courtyard stair open, beckoning us to follow. All the while I think about the relic from the Holy Land, the only thing which gives my Lady hope. The most valuable thing in the castle; I heard Lord Maxwell say so himself.

I am certain now: it's down there in the tunnel, wrapped in velvet cloth and ready to be sold to line De Berclay's pockets.

I am looking into Squire Graham's eyes, begging him silently not to walk away. He can't possibly understand, but maybe he'll trust me. I gesture at the tunnel and make a beckoning motion with my hands, followed by clasping them together in a silent plea.

Godfrey looks flabbergasted betwixt me and the Squire, but then he understands and looks for a hiding place behind stacked barrels. I join him.

It is amazing how much the prisoner can distort his voice; he sounds remarkably like De Berclay when he calls down the tunnel. 'She's heavy. Come back and aid me in hiding the body for a minute.'

There is a groan from further along the tunnel, followed by clinking and a rattle. The Squire makes sure he stands well back, ready with his sword. A head appears. 'Commander De Berclay, we must make haste or else we'll—'

But the henchman never gets to finish what he was going to say: I've slung my apron across his eyes and

Colban Graham presses his sword against the man's neck.

'Climb up,' he snarls into the man's ear, who has no choice but to obey.

'Sit,' he growls again, and De Berclay's henchman whimpers, but follows the order. Squire Graham hands me his belt to tie the man's arms and I pull it tight with all my might. 'There. Secure,' I say. Godfrey has found a length of rope for his feet and the Squire sees to a gag.

The candles on the walls flicker and we hear a rumble in the distance, followed by shouting and a crash, which makes the ground shake for a moment.

'They are using the siege engines to bombard the Gatehouse,' Colban Graham explains. 'Where does this tunnel lead? Outside?'

'I think it must.'

'A secret passage out of the castle…' I can see it in the Squire's face: the hope of escape. He could throw himself on the mercy of the enemy—if they don't kill him at first sight.

It's risky.

But it's probably the only choice he has.

'There is something very precious to my Lady in there. I'll come with you, to retrieve it.'

With that, I wrench one of the candles off the wall and drop myself into the blackness of the tunnel, followed by the beltless Knight. 'Keep watch, Godfrey. If anything happens, keep yourself safe.'

The dampness of the walls and the complete silence of the earth is almost overwhelming. It is easier for me to feel my way ahead of the prisoner, unencumbered by armour or weapons. Soon I reach a hollowed-out chamber where the sacks of coins and jewels rest against the earthen wall. On top of it is the velveteen parcel. I rush to check. The ring is tucked into an embroidered pocket on its own, and the rest is wrapped around the vase from the Holy Land, yet unbroken. How my heart dances at that. I've longed to touch it before and a tingle of excitement ripples through my fingers as I do.

'I will attempt it.'

I had momentarily forgotten all about the Knight behind me. In fact, I had forgotten most of what was in my mind just a moment before. I press my back against the chamber wall to let him past. There is a small chink of light ahead, now that I look properly. With rock and dripping earth above me, I shelter the candle as best as I can while attempting to sling my arm around the sack, which is much heavier that I thought it would be.

'God be with you,' I whisper after him. His receding figure blocks out most of the distant light.

I slide the ring onto my finger, cradle the vase against my body with my elbow and struggle back to where Godfrey is keeping watch. It can't be more than a hundred paces, but in the narrow passage, every ell feels like a league. From time to time I half-turn to strain for the light beyond the moat where Colban Graham will make good his escape—or die. My prayers travel after him in the tunnel, while the attacks and counterattacks above me carry on. All is dulled here; it is like a grave. Slowly, slowly, I progress, wary of unsettling the earth around me, or of alerting anyone to my presence. At one point, I hear metal upon metal in the far distance beyond the castle and half-expect Edward's army to make their way into Caerlaverock after me, ambushing my Lord's men from within.

But then I am knocked off my feet by a blast so huge and so loud that for a moment, I don't know which way is up or down. My candle has gone out and I am alerted by the slow and silent rill of small stones from the roof of the tunnel, just ahead of me, followed by a groaning of the earth. I am paralysed for a second, but then I scramble forward as the tunnel beyond me caves before my very eyes, with earth and mud and rock falling all about me. I can't be sure, but the castle cellar is this way, is it not? I have not time to dither or to satisfy myself I'm right—any dallying will result in being buried alive.

I don't trust my mind, or my heart—I put all my faith in my legs, which seem to know what to do even now as they squelch through sodden mud. My free arm shovels and the other still cradles the sack and the vase to my stomach. While my lungs have a little air I will dig, I will

crawl, I will drag, I will survive, oh holy God.
   I will survive and not die unconfessed and unblessed.

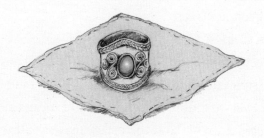

16

DUST AND MUD

I breathe in dust and mud. There is nothing else. Dust and mud crunches in my mouth, my ears. I close my eyes and try to control my mind to keep the panic at bay. I wonder if the prisoner did make it out, and I wonder how Godfrey fares. Godfrey! He might be my only hope. I stop my panicked scratching at earth and wait, wishing the throbbing in my ears to cease.

Yes!

There in the distance, I hear my name.

'Ada! Ada, are you safe?'

'Tis high-pitched and fearful, and dulled by earth, but it comes from…

'ADA!'

That way! I summon my resolve and dig; dig because my life depends on it. The thought that the precious relic is with me lends me strength, and I hear grunting and thudding noises from the other side, too: Godfrey is trying to free the way for me.

It feels like ten lifetimes, but slowly and surely, his voice becomes clearer, more distinct.

'I'm coming, Godfrey. Help me.'

I feel fatigue setting in and panic clutches at my lungs, squeezing and wringing them like a mud-sodden sheet. Every handful of rock and mud means a handful less betwixt myself and the cellar, myself and the light, myself and life. I can't see, but my whole sense is directed to the small, frightened voice and the scraping sounds from the other side. Hot blood trickles down my scratched hands—I can feel it. 'I can't go on, Godfrey,' I try to shout, but it comes out more like a whimper. With a sudden thud, the mud above me collapses, crumbling around my head and I crumple, folding my battered body around the treasures. Prayers half-form in my mind, and I expect the Angel of the Lord to escort me to Purgatory where, at best, I'll reside for half the next eternity, with no one saying masses for me. Instead, I feel a tearing at my hair. 'Lift your head up, Ada, I command thee! Ada, move! Come on, Ada!'

Godfrey cradles my head in his arms, wipes my nose of dust and mud with his tabard, and I open my mouth to gulp in the stale cellar air. Again and again I cough, spitting out mud and stones, dust and water.

'Blessings on you, Godfrey. Help me out of here, I prithee.' The words come out as if I am chewing gravel, but he appears to understand and pulls me up gently. As soon as I attempt to stand, my legs fail again, and I fall backwards onto the tied-up and gagged henchman who groans in protest. I nearly laugh.

'Try again!' For an eight-year-old, Godfrey has authority, make no mistake.

'You'll make a good Knight someday, Godfrey.' I grunt as I finally heave myself to my feet.

'Got to survive this day first,' he grunts back, straining under my weight as he helps me keep balance. Only then I notice that the cellar wall has caved in alarmingly.

Godfrey's mouth twitches. 'The siege engine must have struck above. We need to get out, and fast.'

The bent wall creaks and groans; I try not to think of the weight of Caerlaverock's curtain wall bearing down on it. Up, up the stairs and out of here. With every step, I send a brief prayer of thanks to the Almighty, and beg protection for Colban Graham who has suffered enough injustice. Suddenly I stop.

'What about him there?' I ask Godfrey, gesturing back to where the henchman lies.

Godfrey groans, but his heart is noble, for he turns immediately.

The boy may not yet have the strength to wield a proper sword, but he has a dirk, and by heaving together, we manage to pull the man upright and cut the ties around his legs only, leaving his hands bound. He tries to curse through his gag, which would be funny if the situation wasn't so serious. Apart from that, there is something else which occupies my mind greatly. Halfway up the stair, when the fog in my mind has cleared sufficiently, I pull on Godfrey's tabard.

'Godfrey, did I imagine it, or was Commander De Berclay not lying in the cellar unconscious before all of this?'

In the daylight filtering down into the staircase now, I watch the blood drain from his face. 'By all the holy relics in the realm! I had nothing else to tie him up with, and when the tunnel collapsed—'

He must have taken his chance. Nausea crashes over me, but also a strange determination. 'Tis just possible that the prisoner made it out of the castle alive and undetected. One life saved, and for that I cannot be sorry. I will return the treasure to the Lady Maxwell and explain everything.

Barely able to walk, I clutch the sack and parcel holding the Lord Maxwell's gold while pressing the precious relic to my heart. We halt at the corner of the courtyard, leading the cursing henchman. Rushing towards us is the Lady Maxwell herself, flanked by her aunt—and De Berclay whose face bears witness to its collision with the dirty door.

'Milady, here is the man!' De Berclay points to the henchman. Speaking makes him wince, at which I smile a little, but my amusement is banished by the look of sheer ice from his bloodshot eyes. 'The scoundrel I was telling you about, milady. Trying to make off with your treasure in the heat of a siege battle, how despicable a sin is that! I was trying to locate him—this is why I have been absent from proceedings. I was sure you would value your property, especially the relic.'

The Lady Maxwell rushes forward and slaps the henchman across the face twice. I flinch, because what's next is logical, and I do not know how avert it! Surely, De Berclay is going to accuse us of being accomplices and thieves, which will get us locked up—possibly killed.

Godfrey, however, finds his tongue before me. 'Milady, God save you. We were following the Commander into the cellar when we realised—'

De Berclay interrupts. 'When they realised that I needed help. These children have been invaluable in helping me catch the villain, milady, and I ask with respect that they would be rewarded when the enemy has abandoned the siege.'

Godfrey and I stare, speechless. He is cleverer than I gave him credit for! If we are locked up and guarded, we are also protected. However, if we are free to roam the castle and so is De Berclay...

'Thank you, Commander. You are needed at the Gatehouse now. Do not leave your post again or my husband shall hear of it. Have the damage inspected and repaired. If the cellar wall needs to come down, then let us give the King's army a taste of their own medicine.'

She stares at me until I realise. Holding my arms out and allowing the aunt to take the sack from my bleeding hands, I curtsey as best as my scratched and wobbly legs allow. Godfrey bows. Her eyes linger on the precious ring, still on my finger.

'Oh yes, milady—I was trying to keep it safe. Forgive me.'

Even through the grime, its splendour sparkles as I wrestle it off my swollen hand. 'Tis a wide, solid band in warm, coppery gold with fine wrought-work in spiral patterns, curled around a precious stone set securely into its middle.

Glimmers of greed appear in De Berclay's eyes when I pass it to him, and he, reluctantly, hands it to the Lady Maxwell.

She looks determined in the daylight of the courtyard. The siege must bring unbearable pressure on so young a mistress, but for now it doesn't show. 'Now go, both of you. No pair of hands can be spared. Come, Commander De Berclay. We have business to attend to.'

With this, the Lady of the Castle turns and walks away towards her quarters with De Berclay skulking behind her like a chastened child. Godfrey gives me a half-smile and joins the sentries. Gradually, I become aware again of the shouting outside the castle walls, the whizzing of rocks and the exhausted and desperate movements of our own soldiers.

Dragging myself to my father's kitchen, I sink down onto the chair by the range where he enfolds me in a warm embrace as soon as he returns. A large vat of oil is heating again over the fire and I try to steel myself for what must inevitably follow.

17

POURING SCORN

Fa doesn't normally show the strain, but his face is lined with more than dust today. His eyes are crusted with salt and there are smears across his apron. Bloody smears; smears of pain.

'Old Sir Walter Weir?' I ask.

He clears his throat, awkwardly. 'I won't deny it, Ada. My soul is sore. I wish his spirit could have clung on. But I am glad that the Friar was with him. There may be more in need of last rites and confessions before long.' As if the enemy camp had heard him, there is another crash, followed by crumbling, splintering and shouting. 'You look a sight, Ada. What happened to you?' Fa turns his back and stirs the oil; it mustn't catch fire in the kitchen.

Even speaking is painful, and how could I possibly tell him all? All the mouths in the kingdom and all the time in the world would not be enough to tell all.

I groan instead, and he nods, acknowledging it is

enough. A man of few words. How often I have wished that he was different, but right now I am only grateful. However, I also realise something. *What use is lying still and dwelling on my plight? I am getting stiffer and the pain threatens to claim the last of my resolve. Will I allow my brain to cloud with self-pity and despair? Is this what the good God brought me out of the tunnel for? Is this what Godfrey risked his life for?*

It is NOT!

I grind my teeth together, gather up my stained shift and push myself upwards. Reaching for the bucket of water and a clean apron by the range, I splash my face, dry it with my sleeve and then wipe my hands and feet. If today is the day we all face our Maker, let my hands not be idle.

'What needs done, Fa?'

He smothers the flames to keep the oil from overheating and turns.

'Everything needs to be done, and at the same time, nothing can be done. It is out of our hands, Ada. The Lady Maxwell and Commander De Berclay will judge best whether we can hold out against such a force. From my heart, I wish our Lord Maxwell was back in these walls.'

I can only sigh. 'Give me something to do Fa, or I'll go moonstruck. Without a task, my hands will only shake and shake.'

He holds my gaze longer than usual. 'At times like these, men and girls are the same. Fearful. But onwards, Ada, shout for the Squires. The oil is ready!'

I call up to the ramparts. The oldest Squire comes first, but I am astonished to see his face, blood-streaked and scratched, his fine clothes torn beneath broken armour. Despite all that, he walks with energy and purpose, like a nobleman should.

'We have made this.' He motions for another Squire to come in. Between them, they carry an odd-looking wooden contraption.

The Squire demonstrates, hoisting the ends of two long planks onto his shoulders while his companion does the same. The makeshift tray betwixt them rises. Ah, now I understand. The wooden carrier strikes me as sturdy enough, despite only being tied together with lengths of twisted rope. Fa dons his thick leather gloves and closes his hands around the rim of the pot.

'Careful!' I jump forward, wrapping my own hands in my apron, and guide the full vessel towards the tray.

'Keep watch. Because if it tips...' My father's voice is more groan that instruction, but his tension soon settles on us all. If this boiling oil spills on us instead of them, eternity will be upon us in a moment. If we manage to funnel it out through the slit in the castle wall, the same will be true of our enemies. A twinge of concern distracts me. The Knights who are attacking us are under obligation to their King—that is even more true of the foot soldiers and archers launching rock after rock at our castle. They have no choice, just as we have no choice. All *they* can do is follow orders and act with bravery and chivalry. All that remains for *us* to do is to defend our castle with more of the same.

The young men hesitate as the enormity of the risk filters into their humour. The leader of the Squires begins. The burning hot vessel rests on his shoulders, separated from his skin only by the strips of wood. Guided by me, he takes small steps. 'Heat more oil, cook. 'Tis the express instruction of Commander De Berclay. Maid, guide us!'

They stare at the pot, not on their path. My eyes have to be their eyes now; I must stay close. Still, arrows fly overhead. Suddenly, there is a collective shout above us on the battlements, and at the same time, a piercing metallic clang echoes from the castle gate. Our precious cargo sways.

'Wait! Stay still, for the love of God, and let the liquid settle!' In no ordinary time could I have spoken thus sharply to a Squire, but they obey, steadying their gait until I have righted the pot. The short walk to the Gatehouse feels like a league, but we reach it with only small drops of the liquid sizzling on the straw-covered ground.

'Careful now.' Each step up the stone staircase is

perilous, but soon we reach the portcullis chamber with its narrow slits. One of De Berclay's guards stands beside it, risking an occasional glance down.

He nods at the hot liquid which the two Squires are now guiding, carefully, towards the window slit. Oh, that is clever! One end of their wooden contraption sits on the stone floor—it allows them to tip it without exposing themselves to danger—they can simply stand on either side of the window and tilt.

The guard lifts up a piece of metal armour. I can't tell what it once was, but it has been beaten into a funnel shape and the guard holds it beneath the rim of the vessel.

'Now!' commands the Squire.

It isn't a slick or elegant movement, but betwixt us, we manage to direct the burning liquid into the funnel and through the castle wall, pouring it onto the entrance directly beneath us.

We hold our breath.

18

SILENCE

Fa curses as he hears the clashing and rattling of retreating metal: we have missed! Even our archers from the battlements can't shoot down now as they are under renewed attack themselves. We duck as a separate volley of crossbow arrows find the slit. Some of the hot oil pools at our feet.

'It doesn't matter,' mumbles the guard. 'It sends the message that we won't surrender. That we are going to do whatever is necessary to defend ourselves. That was the Lady of the Castle's instruction.'

I think of her, the Lady—walking as if a westerly wind could undo her, slight perhaps, but steadfast too, like the golden threads wound into her scarlet robe.

'What does the Commander say?' Father snaps. He sounds tired and irritable to me, but aren't we all?

The guard shrugs. 'De Berclay will respond to the enemies' provocations. Just as they will respond to ours.'

A horn sounds outside.

Fa's face falls—so has the guard's.

The Squires have turned to each other, standing stock-still.

'Hark!' Fa whispers. I strain to listen.

Nothing.

None of us are breathing and I cannot fathom why. Until I realise—the silence *is* the reason.

The enemy has stopped bombarding us with missiles. Their archers and foot soldiers are withdrawing up the hill to their camp where they form a cordon—but I can see them sitting down to rest, too.

Now that the danger from archers seems to be gone, we crowd around the narrow slit. Our drawbridge is still up, although the English army have felled trees and laid the trunks across the moats by way of a bridge.

I can hear De Berclay's voice from the top of the Gatehouse, summoning his soldiers and I instinctively recoil. *Where is Godfrey now?*

I catch Fa casting me a sideways glance. 'The Lady will need sustenance, Ada. See to it.'

My father is like that—as soon as he is caught *feeling*, he *does something*. Anything. *Doing* banishes the feeling, and if I had lost a wife in childbirth and been left with only a daughter instead of an heir, I might be the same. There is nothing to forgive.

'Yes, Fa.' I bow my head and run up the servant

stairs to my own quarters. My father's bedclothes lie in disarray, hurriedly abandoned. I pull off my sodden shift and bring out my Sunday one from under the bed. I do not wish to spoil it, but I cannot go on in this soaked garment else I want to catch my death and put my humours out of balance for good.

It amazes me, but I feel like a new person, dipping my dirty hands into the horses' trough before returning to the kitchen.

I have watched Fa often enough to know what to do. A girl in charge in a castle kitchen! Whatever next? But no one gives me a second glance today. I fan the embers on the range into flames, add some wood and begin a quick stew of barley and fish. The spices entice me, but I can't waste them with my inexperience, so salt and a little pepper will have to suffice, along with some parsley from the herb pot on the windowsill. I am distraught that the enemy troops can help themselves to all the produce from the kitchen garden outside the castle walls now. But there is nothing I can do about it. Running back to the partially caved-in cellar to fetch wine, I assemble the bowl on a tray, add a goblet and steady myself. I need to be careful of the Commander. I can hardly blame him—I know enough to see him hanged. The problem is, no one will believe me, and he will want to put that beyond doubt. I resolve to bolt the door every night and praise the Almighty that I am still sharing a bedchamber with my father whose muscles are thrice the volume of De Berclay's. If I ever do get to lie down in my bed again, that is. Oh, it's all too much for my mangled mind. One thing at a time. The one thing at *this* time is to carry the food to the Lady Maxwell.

The wooden treads of the staircase creak, and I nearly miss my footing where a tread has splintered asunder; no doubt a stone missile landed on it. I catch my balance just in time and scurry up towards the Great Hall where the Lady is kneeling at her altar to pray. The Friar intones the final *Amen*. She crosses herself and rises as my steps approach. 'Go, Friar Malcolm, and see if they have need of you.'

He looks a little grey in the face. Maybe even such a man of God can feel fear. He mumbles his assent, smiles at me briefly and disappears through the heavy curtains to the main stair.

I place the tray in front of her seat at the table.

'Thank you. You may stay.' Her voice trembles but a little, and I am struck anew at her strength. It is still uncannily quiet outside.

The Lady inclines her head towards me: 'The silence of three thousand men or more is much more unnerving than their war-cries, is it not?'

"Tis, milady.'

'Their catapults have not breached the walls of our great castle.'

I look around. *Where are her ladies-in-waiting? Her aunt?*

She has read my mind. 'They have chosen to remain in their chambers. They prefer not to see the King's army beleaguering us here.'

I do not know what to say to that. Eventually, I answer. 'Caerlaverock is strong, milady.'

'Yes, but I am alone. No husband to guide me, no friends to cheer me.' I turn to look over my shoulder, but the Lady Maxwell is talking to *me*, that much is clear. She doesn't look at me though—maybe speaking to a laundress *and* looking at her is more than she can consciously stoop to.

A sharp knock on the door startles us both. She takes a deep breath and makes a show of drinking her fish stew as soon as she has commanded: 'Enter!'

It's him, of course it is. His steps halt for a moment when he sees me. The Lady misinterprets. 'Do not mind her, Commander. She came to serve me, and I bid her stay and wait on me.'

'Very well.' De Berclay turns his back on me.

Oh, how I wish I could remain in the presence of the Lady of the Castle for evermore. De Berclay could not assault me in her presence, could he? I wonder that neither of the adults in the room enquire after the sound of my knees, knocking into one another with fear, or the thunder of my beating heart, high up in my throat.

'Lady Maxwell, it appears that the direct attack has ceased. We inspected the damage on the walls, and aside from some shifting earth beneath the wine cellar...'

He means the collapsed tunnel.

'...there is no major breach yet. Two of the young Knights have injuries, and we have lost five archers. Old Sir Walter Weir... you know about him. Other than that, I have instructed that fifteen return to their quarters for a rest while the rest of us keep watch, ready to alert them at a moment's notice. I fear the onslaught is not over yet.'

'Commander De Berclay, you need not patronise me. I have been observing the landing of much wood over the course of the morning. There is but one thing to do—show the enemy how little effect their attack is having—I will show myself as a sign of our nonchalance. Do accompany me.'

She has barely touched her food, but rises and walks up the staircase, with De Berclay urging caution in her wake. I don't know what comes over me, but I abandon the half-eaten bowl of stew on the table and sneak after them.

19

THE COURAGE OF A LADY

I haven't been up here on the battlements for some time—the sea of mingling men ebbs and flows before my eyes. The view of the sweeping landscape alone normally strikes awe into my heart, but how different the hill looks, cloaked in colour like this. I get a much better view of the shields and banners, displaying the various Knights' crests, the flags and royal guards, the horses' saddle blankets and the sheets and bunting fluttering in the summer breeze. Standing here, I feel insignificant, like a margin mark in a chronicle. History is being made in this very place at this very moment. Below us is nothing but strength and ease. Up here, despite the Lady's defiance, there is only exhaustion.

The Lady of the Castle bears the sight with fortitude. She takes her kerchief from the folds of her long sleeves, her veil and wimple fluttering in the wind. Down in the enemy camp, I see soldiers pointing as a communal murmur rumbles through the air—they have seen her. The Lady smiles, stretches and begins to wave her kerchief above the battlements, as is she is merely dusting, letting the King of England know that he is not doing any damage of note. De Berclay's face is inscrutable, as if he doesn't know what to make of this Lady Maxwell and her determination.

'Your missiles and rams cannot break our defences. Pack up and go to trouble another Border-Lord!' The Lady says it audibly, but how can the army below possibly hear it? Then I realise—she is saying it for us, for the Squires and the guards, the soldiers and their Commander, for the fearful Friar, for me and the rest of the servants, and yes, possibly even for herself. We must not lose heart. *She* must not lose heart.

With a sweeping flash of her sleeves, she turns and makes for the stairs back down into the Great Hall, and I am quick to scurry down ahead of her, moving the cold half-eaten stew away and refilling her goblet.

She sits at the table. 'They will leave, Commander. Why else have they withdrawn this far and allowed us to rest. I am confident. We will hold out until my husband returns.'

'Milady, I wish I could share your faith, but—'

She waves him away. There is a shout from the watcher above us on the battlements. '*Rider!*'

'Check.' The Lady nods in my direction, and I

carefully lean into the arrow slit window to see. Quick as a whip I twitch my head back again—and only just in time. The goblet of expensive wine spills across the table, splashing its red liquid all over De Berclay's hose. The goblet slides into his lap and then clatters to the floor. There—embedded in the wood of the table and just below my Lady's trembling hand—is an arrow.

'What remarkable aim that archer has,' croaks De Berclay grudgingly, and I can't help agreeing with him, now that I know my Lady isn't hurt. 'They must know that these are the Lord Maxwell's quarters. But milady! There is a message, wrapped around the arrow.' The Commander reaches for it, but the Lady gets there first. She is of the highest rank, and I have heard that she reads both French and Latin.

'They offer us free passage if we abandon the castle.' Her voice sounds like a child's, full of wonder.

'Well, with only sixty men we cannot hope to hold out long. Perhaps we should consider—'

'Silence!' roars the Lady, and for a moment, I turn to see whether that utterance could have come from anyone else. But no, the Lady's face is set.

'Commander, we have held out for a day and a night. We shall hold out for many more, as long as I am the Lady of the Castle and as long as my Lord is away from home. I will hold out, do you hear, until the walls crumble around me. I cannot surrender. My husband has instructed me not to.'

The Commander lowers his head. 'Erm, milady, the rider is still standing betwixt us and his own army. He might be waiting.'

'Waiting, is he? Well, do not leave him in any doubt of our response!'

Some minutes later, the engineer of the castle crouches beneath the top of the battlements, readying the catapult—the only one within the castle walls. A stone, circular and shiny, has been fixed on it, wrapped in the Lady Maxwell's message.

I hope the King is not of too delicate a composition, for I am told that the Lady of the Castle has used language most unladylike in her response, composed entirely in French—one of the Squires heard her read it aloud.

The catapult lever snaps, the rope uncoils—and our message of defiance flies out into the air above Caerlaverock before thudding hard into the ground, not ten yards from the waiting rider. We can see the dust explode into the air. The watching Friar, who has joined us again in the Great Hall, grimaces and cradles his dog Nosewise into his lap.

Once again, the dice are cast.

'The Lord God preserve us all,' the Friar mutters beside me.

20

WISE COUNSEL

It doesn't take long. The aggression outside pulses like a wound, oozing and angry, all around Caerlaverock.

We watch from the window. The Friar, the Lady and me.

Their envoy picks up our letter, torn a little by the impact—we can see that even from here—and rides back. I can only assume that it is the King he takes our message to. Our catapult never had the range to do damage to their army, but now they move forward together, crowding around something large. A man, who may or may not be an engineer, directs the action and huge pieces of wood rise into the air and slot into one another. Balanced by a spider's web of ropes and chains, it assembles and rolls towards us, a siege tower! I have heard bards sing of these things. Outside, we hear De Berclay bark his instructions to whoever will listen. 'Arrows, fiery ones, right now. This instant—what are you waiting for? What are you WAITING for? Do it, man! You there, wake every man capable of wielding a sword. In fact, wake the weaklings as well. Go!'

I'm mesmerised—the siege tower is almost the height of our castle wall and is covered in animal skins; there is no way of knowing how many men it can conceal within. While I've been distracted by that, I've neglected keeping an eye on what has been going on below us by the moat.

'Stay down!'

The Lady herself pulls me back, but not before I saw it: a huge battering ram, covered by a leather roof so their men are protected from our arrows. All they need to do now is to get it across the moat.

'There!' croaks the Friar and I barely can summon the courage to follow his outstretched arm. The advancing army is assembling a trebuchet—a TREBUCHET— which is being pulled into existence by thirty men or more. Up and up it rises until I cannot possibly imagine it rising any more. In its sling I can see a rock the size of half a horse. *It cannot be done! Can it?*

Where are they aiming it?

The Lady herself stands up flagpole straight and raises her dusty kerchief up to her forehead. In wiping it, she smears smoky earth and dust right across—like battle paint—but she is unaware, and I haven't the heart to tell her.

A writing mass of armed men continues to disappear into the siege tower. Soon the tower itself begins to move slowly. Is it rolling forward towards the castle? Or is it a trick of the eye? No, I'm certain now: it is truly moving towards us. It feels wrong, somehow, that the sky is still blue. Men in their hundreds beat their swords against their shields, and if it is meant to intimidate us, it is working.

Orders are barked from the battlements. 'All men to arms! Send someone to keep watch on the postern gate; they have enough soldiers to make an attempt in both places! Boy, go to the back and keep watch there. But careful—don't lean over the wall and be sure to shout if anything is amiss.'

Boy? Boy? Can that be...

'I wish they wouldn't train the Pages so young,' the Lady's aunt whispers. She looks gaunt and tired. So quietly did she enter the room that I didn't even hear her come in.

In passing, I grab the Lady's cold plate and thunder down the wooden stairs into the courtyard. 'Godfrey, wait!' I shout. 'I'm coming with you. Wait for me! Godfrey, wait!'

He is ahead of me. And then it happens—the giant rock roars through the air above me, overtakes me and smashes into the East Tower. The noise throbs in my ears. Both of us stagger back, glare at each other in fright and scramble to our feet again. They have seen it from the Gatehouse; they must have seen. The walls of the East Tower sway, stilled for a mere moment by an invisible hand, before the structure bends a little, and the top half of it disappears, swallowed in a dusty gulp by the lower part. My mouth hangs open. Dust and grime settle on my tongue, but for now I'm paralysed.

'Ada, come on.'

He is not seriously suggesting standing on the battlements to keep watch after this, surely?

It would appear he is. 'Ada, I must follow an order.'

'But it's madness, Godfrey. You'll die, and what's to be gained by that? Sometimes the *world* changes. Then we must think for ourselves!'

My lips are cracking, such is the urgency with which I speak. Desperate shouting from the Gatehouse confirms that the siege tower is upon the castle walls, with De Berclay and his men firing at it from every possible angle.

Think for ourselves…

I should heed my own words!

'Godfrey. Holding out against this is hopeless. Hopeless.'

Both of us are thrown off our feet by the impact of another massive rock which smashes into the Eastern Curtain wall of the castle, denting it badly.

'I know,' he whispers miserably, and I realise that before me is simply an eight-year-old boy who is not ready to die. His brows are pinched, his skin almost translucently pale, and he shivers.

The castle wall creaks alarmingly. *What if the next blow brings it down?*

'Come on, Godfrey. We're are going to see the Lady.'

We find her in the Lord's Hall, all alone. In the next room, the Friar is in the middle of conducting some sort of mass for her aunt and the ladies-in-waiting. Nosewise howls loudly, but his master pays him no heed.

Below us, nearly within arrowshot, is an army of warriors, tasked with bringing this castle down, and us with it. Even now, rubble falls past the arrow slots. Above us, out of sight on the ramparts of the Gatehouse Tower, we hear metal on metal, sword upon sword. The siege tower has done its work and they are upon us. No wonder she hasn't heard us enter.

'Milady.'

Still she remains unmoved, standing at an angle to conceal herself from the enemy, while retaining a view of onslaught on all sides.

I clear my throat to speak. *This goes against everything I have been taught. Don't be seen, don't be heard. Never directly address the Maxwell family.*

Know your place.

My voice rings out as clear as a bell.

'Lady Maxwell. May I speak with you?'

She slowly turns round at that and looks me up and

down. I see a fresh trail of salty tears down her cheek, and at that moment I understand that we are not so different after all.

'Lady Maxwell, the destruction of the castle is…' I try to think of a clever word, but it will not come. 'We cannot hold out; I'm certain of it.'

'I know.' Her voice is small. Barely there. The outside noise is dulled by the thick walls, or else I'd hear nothing of her words at all.

'Milady, will you surrender? For the good of the men under your patronage?'

She glances out through the arrow slit again, as if considering whether to deign to reply. Below, we hear something like chanting—the battering ram is across the moat, it would seem. Soon it will advance. Engineers are in the process of setting up the giant trebuchet once more. I feel sick.

'I can't.' Her answer is no more than a whimper.

'Why not?' That came out much more insolent than I meant it to. I drop my volume. 'With respect, why not, milady?'

'My husband left me with instructions not to give up the castle, whatever happens. I am a wife. I must obey my—'

'But that makes no sense!'

I spin round. 'Godfrey, you can't speak to the Lady like that!' Turning to the Lady Maxwell again, I continue.

'But he's right, milady. Your husband, God protect him, is not here. You are. You need to decide. Yourself. You are the only one who can end this.'

She turns her back to us.

'Leave me,' she snaps.

Defeated, we walk away. Outside, panicked footsteps batter the wooden stairs as men flee battlements and hide from the impact of the missiles.

Something like a sob rocks the Lady, but her voice is steady when she speaks again, just before we leave the hall.

'Halt. Fetch me a flag, a white banner. Anything will do.'

I think more quickly this time. 'My apron? It isn't exactly clean, but—'

'Yes, hand it to me. And fetch Commander De Berclay. I must speak with him, urgently.'

Fetch De Berclay?

No. Not me.

I simply can't.

21

THE LEADER AND THE LED

'We'll do it together, Ada, out in the open,' says Godfrey, 'Then he can't do a thing.'

I'm almost embarrassed at how terrified I am of a mere man, when flying missiles and fiery weapons could end my life in the blink of an eye. Godfrey is right, of course he is.

We have just stepped out when a crash rents the air and splinters fly. The wooden stair, which leads directly from the Great Hall to the courtyard, has been hit!

We are trapped!

A young soldier lies beneath the smashed pieces of wood, and his companions are running towards him, pulling him out. 'Tis a drop, but I reckon we could jump it.

'Where is the Commander?' I shout, but the men ignore me. Louder, I scream: 'Where is Commander De Berclay? We have a message from the Lady Maxwell. He is to see her urgently!'

Something like hope flickers from one gaze to the other. These men, like us, have lost faith in holding out, but they must, if it is the Lord's and Lady's will. She may yet save our lives, all of us, if she surrenders. Of course, the King of England could have us all killed for resisting in the first place. It's a risk. If we surrender, we *may* die. If we don't, we *will* die.

'The Commander, quickly!'

The message passes betwixt voices, faster than fire betwixt dry reeds. High on the Eastern Wall, I detect him now, standing upright. A soldier runs up to him, others fetch a ladder so he can descend.

'The Lady requires you now,' Godfrey offers, avoiding the Commander's gaze. I have withdrawn into a gap betwixt two pillars, hoping De Berclay won't notice me and pass me by. But it is in vain.

He stops, his face hardens in a mask of self-control. I almost feel sorry for him for a moment. None of his plans have worked, and he finds himself in a confrontation he cannot win, tasked with holding up outdated wishes from an absent Lord. My pity doesn't last long.

'Just you wait,' he hisses under his breath. Then turning and speaking more clearly, he declares, 'Take me to her.'

I walk ahead of him. Godfrey struggles to keep up with the Commander's powerful strides, which just serves to highlight how young he is, and how small.

I expect De Berclay to attempt to sway the Lady, or to make it look like his own idea, but the Lady has washed her face and stands up straight. 'Commander, take this.'

The authority in her voice startles De Berclay into stretching out his hands and receiving my dirty apron.

'But milady—'

'I have made up my mind,' she says, and her voice doesn't falter. 'Lower it from the ramparts. I am certain now.'

'It is too dangerous. There is hand-to-hand combat up there.'

Just then, a giant missile hits the Gatehouse, just below the Great Hall. The room shakes. The Lady loses her balance slightly, and De Berclay has to steady her. Stone dust rains past the windows and puffs out of the cracks inside.

As soon as she can stand, she strides across to the fireplace where the fire has long gone out—all the servants are busy defending the fortress—and pulls down a ceremonial lance mounted above.

'Then tie our flag to this and wave it above the battlements. If you are not man enough to do it yourself, then I most certainly will. I simply will not risk more life and limb within these walls. If this displeases my husband, I shall deal with his displeasure at our next encounter. Go henceforth!'

'Milady.' The nod could not have been curter, the bow not shallower. His voice croaks a little. For a second, I worry he is not going to obey the Lady's instructions—it must have crossed his mind. She has thought of it too, for she hastens after him and cries through the open doorway and into the courtyard: 'I, Lady Agnes Maxwell, have instructed our Commander to SURRENDER. A white flag shall be flown above the castle. Everyone is to disarm, do you hear? Raise the portcullis and lower the drawbridge. I have made this decision of my own free will and will defend it to anyone who dares question it. Do as I say, by the authority of my husband the Lord Maxwell himself, do not delay. Do as I say.'

Her face is flushed when she turns to face us and there is a new energy in her step. I smile, and for the briefest of moments, I fancy she smiles back, tight like a bowstring.

Two more impacts strike down by the side of the Gatehouse Tower, but then, oh my Lord, can it be true? A lone horn is blown. Its welcome sound is soon joined by many others. Is that the sound of surrender? I risk a peek through the small slit and I see nothing but calm blue sky. Their giant trebuchet, halfway through re-loading, is abandoned by its engineers. But the danger isn't over; chivalry and trickery are never far apart in these Borderlands. Then I hear the creak of the drawbridge. Godfrey and I run out of the hall and climb down the damaged stairs—yes!—the drawbridge is coming down.

Small and steady is the movement, but the first proper view of what we were up against at ground level is overwhelming—so many legs and arms and helmets, I can barely disentangle each fighter in my mind. There is a rattle and a creak—the wheel for the portcullis is turning, though the men barely have the strength to pull the chain.

Above me, the Lady of the Castle appears, picking her steps down the stair carefully, and two Squires rush to help her over the damaged part. I am suddenly self-conscious, standing in the courtyard alone with Godfrey. Soon, though, they begin to arrive on all sides: servants, Squires, soldiers and stable boys. Swords, hurriedly thrown down, begin to form a pile.

The Lady looks so strange and so beautiful out in the open air, with her almost floor-length sleeves and her scarlet velvet dress. She inclines her head to De Berclay. 'It has to be me, Commander. I will be the one to lead our people out. May the Lord God protect us all.'

Lady Maxwell begins to move. Every step is an act of courage. Through the inner gate. Below the portcullis. I half-expect an arrow to hole her through this instant, such is the cruelty for which the King of England is famous. Ahead of our gaggle of hobbling Knights, bandaged Squires, and servants, she all but glides through the outer gate and onto the drawbridge with her head held high.

22

BEYOND THE CASTLE WALLS

The outer gate is barely holding together, splintered and smashed by their battering ram. It scrapes heavily on the ground as our men attempt to push it open wider. The ground is covered in pieces of metal, wooden debris, and dried blood too. Enemy blood.

There is barely a creak as she strides onto the drawbridge. Beyond all of that, a throbbing, expectant sea of soldiers waits, ready to wash over our defeated castle-dwellers, should their King say the word. The Friar is ahead and Godfrey beside me, attempting to brush down his dishevelled tabard. I turn briefly, squashed on all sides, but there, I spy Fa's hood! What a relief!

Step by step, the Lady with her slender figure goes forward, her hair blowing in the wind, wimple askew and her dress dragging through the churned-up ground. Her movements are slow and rhythmical, as if she is walking towards an altar on her marriage day but it is likely that she is walking towards her death. A large knot has formed in my throat. Whatever happens now is in the hands of the Almighty. From behind, Fa puts a heavy hand on my shoulder and squeezes gently, and we follow our Lady.

There are gasps now: the army outside begin to realise how few of us there were all along. In front of us, the Lady Maxwell has reached the open ground and, in one graceful movement, slides to her knees before the King's army. Like a row of lambs before slaughter, our warriors behind her do the same. Godfrey and I walk beside each other, as equals.

We are souls, caught up in the powers and struggles of others. Soul beside soul before the Almighty. 'Tis this thought that comforts me as I reach the open esplanade where the expanse of soldiers before us mirrors the Solway behind us. *Will a volley of arrows rain down on us to punish our insolence? For resisting and holding out?* I glance at my Lady in front, on her knees, and I wonder if she regrets the dusting of the battlements and her defiance of the King of the realm. I do not concern myself with the power of the mighty, I only wish for an honest and humble life, and I hope I don't ask too much. Still feeling Fa's huge hand on my shoulder, I too sink down on my knees—a castle in submission.

What will happen to Caerlaverock now? What will the Lord Maxwell find on his return?

Before us, the crowds ooze apart until an untidy rip of empty ground appears. Trumpets sound. We dare not move. On a dark brown charger, flanked by outriders on both sides, the King himself approaches.

There is movement in our group—those who were not yet kneeling sink down hurriedly. Again, Fa's hand squeezes me from behind and I try to relax my tightly wound sinews by sheer force of will. All around me, sunken eyes and bruised limbs testify to our ordeal— we have resisted valiantly, and now we must accept defeat and throw ourselves on the mercy of Edward Longshanks, Hammer of the Scots.

The King reins back his horse, a mere stone's throw from where we are kneeling. The Lady remains alone at the front, and it strikes me how easy it would be to throw a hammer or a spear and end this man's cruel reign, right here and now. But we are disarmed, surrounded by more than three thousand armed soldiers. We would be ground to dust in seconds.

The King lowers his own sword and gazes down on us coldly. Executions are bound to follow. Revenge is in the air. Even the horses whinny no more.

The King's voice echoes out over the assembled crowd. He speaks the English, so that all of us can understand, not the French which is so fashionable at court. 'We came so that this rebellious land would submit. Submit you have. The castle has fallen to the Crown of England as the Almighty would have it. You deserve death—'

Most of us twitch a little at this.

'But you will be shown mercy. I am your King and only wish to reign in a peaceful and obedient realm. Rebels can expect no such mercy.'

He yells the last part so loudly that the words ricochet round the hillside like stones in an empty pot. It's a threat, make no mistake, to anyone harbouring the rebel William Wallace. I don't dare look around. Would any of us join with Wallace and his rebels, even now?

The King trots his horse around our small huddle. 'Now go and make your homes elsewhere. Remember the grace of your King at a time when you deserved no more than the sword. Tell of this wherever you go.'

It is filtering in, slowly. 'He is going to let us go,' whispers Godfrey. 'I think he truly is going to let us go.'

The King reins his horse in to face us, shouting as much over his shoulder to his own army as down to us: 'I order that new clothes will be given to you in exchange for your armour. Then you shall arise and go.' Behind him, a man is scribbling. Of course, he has a bard with him to tell of the valour of the campaign. I bet those words are going to be in fashionable French.

The King's soldiers begin to move towards us from all sides and, despite the King's words, we recoil into one another. It could be a trap, to avoid any resistance now. At least we are together. I feel Fa's hand squeeze my shoulder again from behind, harder than expected. At the same time, I also feel something else. Something sharp, digging into my back. Something deadly.

How…?

With the arrows of the King's army trained on us still, it would be too risky to turn around. I cast my eyes sideways to look at the hand on my shoulder.

Not a hand scarred with cuts and burns like my father's. No—a hand scarred by battle—like De Berclay's.

As if I needed confirmation, the hand claws into my hair and the dagger he clearly still holds presses hard into my back, in the midst of the huddled crowd.

The words are no more than a snarl, a finger's breadth from my ear. 'You, meddling wretch, are going nowhere without me.'

23

A LIGHTNING PRAYER OF DESPAIR

My throat swells as panic threatens to strangle me. The Commander must have shed his mail and armour and is wearing my father's apron and cloak. The coward has disguised himself to avoid capture and pulled my Fa's hood over his face. No one else seems to be alert to it, too concerned about their own affairs. Even Godfrey hasn't noticed, and I am dying inside. In my ear, I hear another hiss: 'Walk with me, or you shall feel my dagger through your very bowels! No one crosses Brian De Berclay.'

I want to defy him—to raise myself up right here and scream: 'He is armed! The man is armed still, arrest him!' But all my friends from the castle would think I am handing over my father. Where *is* Fa? What has De Berclay done? Paralysed, my mouth slackens, and my helpless hands hang at my side.

The treacherous Commander has lowered his head so that his chin almost touches his chest. That way, nobody will recognise him and point out that he is not the castle cook.

It is then that I spot the blond mane of the prisoner! He is straining to get a look our group—only now he is holding a shield with the Graham family crest, standing beside a broader man with remarkably similar features. His face still bears the bruises from De Berclay's treatment.

Silently, I utter a lightning prayer of despair and the miracle happens—he locks eyes with me, and he points with recognition. His gaze swivels down to Godfrey, slightly ahead of me. I see Colban Graham talking animatedly to those around him, but what hope of help? All I can think of is my Fa, left behind—dead for all I know—and De Berclay's dagger piercing into my back under his cloak. Even over the murmur of the onlookers, I think I can hear my shift tear with the weapon's pressure. How long before he shall make good all his threats? Minutes? Seconds?

We follow the example of the Lady Maxwell who remains kneeling. Dignified and still, she bows her head. Her eyes are closed in petition.

The King's Herald rides out from the crowd. 'It has pleased the King, kind and gracious, to give you new clothes and send you on your way with his blessing. Mercy and grace shall be the mark of his reign. Be therefore loyal subjects to your King. Serve him wholeheartedly.

Long live the King!'

'Long live the King! Long live the King!' The army's chants ring out into the sky, and most of us join in for fear of being held back and punished after all. *Think Ada. Think what to do.*

A handful of officials walk towards us, arms piled high with bundles of folded cloth. The Herald is telling the truth! I take the opportunity to cast a glance backwards, but sixty men and a handful of women are easily scanned and no, my father is definitely not here. De Berclay looks back too but keeps his hood low so that no one but me could possibly recognise his features.

Fa.

My heartbeat is out of control, hammering in my chest, shallow and fast. I feel the fear close around my throat.

'Ada!' Godfrey whispers beside me. 'Ada, are you all right?'

At that precise moment, I cry out under my breath—De Berclay has pushed the knife further into my back, and the material rips for good: a warning. He won't let me give him away now. I don't know why I don't just scream it all out—I am going to die either way. Nevertheless, I nod to Godfrey and smile a forced grimace. It satisfies him. I don't want it to, but it does.

We receive the bundles of clothes in silence, mumbling our thanks.

At the very corner of my vision, I see Squire Graham talk urgently with his relative. He indicates me again. I lower my head. Any attention now will mean the imminent thrust of a dagger into my back

The Herald begins again. 'Now you are free to go. A horse will be provided for the Lady of the Castle by the King's special dispensation. Go now, abandon Caerlaverock and go in peace.'

There is a commotion. The older man, who resembles Colban Graham, makes his way through the crowd and rides up to the side of the Herald, speaking into his ear. For a moment, the Herald seems perplexed, but then his clear, melodic voice rings out one last time.

'As I said, you are free to go. Except—'

He points straight at me and Godfrey, and De Berclay behind me. 'Those three. By order of Sir Hector Graham, Knight and aide to the King, they are to be detained.'

A muttered curse behind me, and I feel the knife slide away from my body, probably up De Berclay's sleeve. Necks are craned at the front, no wonder questioning what the King of England could possibly want with a laundress, a Page boy and a cook. The Friar's face sags with compassion. Even the Lady Maxwell has lifted her head, though her face remains impassive.

I am shaking but manage to get to my feet. Godfrey is properly terrified now, I can tell, especially as the other castle-dwellers stare and mutter amongst themselves.

I look straight ahead as a group of English noblemen, including Colban Graham and his kinsman, ride towards us. On a shiny horse beside our former prisoner sits a young man with the insignia of the royal household who must be the Crown Prince himself. He looks only a little older and I wonder if they could be friends. As soon as I am within earshot, I hear Squire Graham. 'Yes, that man, the one with the hood. I am certain, yes—that is the Castle Commander who tortured me so. Uncle, I assure you, he may well be cowardly enough to disguise himself as a cook. It's him, I'd wager my life on it.'

'Arrest that man! Bring him hither!' thunders the voice of Sir Hector Graham.

Immediately, the soldiers around us grasp the hilts of their swords. De Berclay must realise the game is up and raises his hands in surrender, but he is more dangerous now than he was before—trapped animals are the most lethal of all.

Wait, Godfrey doesn't know who stands behind him! I take my chance to whisper, making sure my hair hides my mouth. 'Godfrey! Watch out because... GODFREY!'

But my friend isn't even listening. 'I didn't tell you, Ada, but my clan is allied with the Bruce. Does the King know that the De Heron clan is rebellious? How could he possibly know that? Ada—'

'Shush, Godfrey. Why would you say that aloud, now of all times?'

His legs buckle and I just catch him, forgetting about De Berclay and poor Fa for a moment. They are here. We bow before the assembled English noblemen.

'That's her. She was my rescuer, Uncle. She and this boy here.'

'Tis the voice of the prisoner again, but not roughened by thirst and strained by pain. He too has been given new clothes, but not the simple garments we now carry. His doublet is velvet and gold. His hair has been trimmed so skilfully that I nearly didn't recognise him. Almost a man, certainly not a boy. An honoured Squire, not a fugitive.

'That man there, on the other hand, Uncle, was my tormentor. He bragged about taking the ransom money without the knowledge of the Lord Maxwell.'

Godfrey looks like nothing in the world makes sense anymore, but then he doesn't know that the man, now flanked by two soldiers, and bowing his head beneath my father's hood, is the Commander.

Colban Graham dismounts and approaches. 'Surrender, scoundrel! Not so high and mighty now, are you?'

There is something I should say, I am sure of it. Everything is so confusing. Fa…

At the very moment, my brain comprehends its duty, I open my lips to shout, and De Berclay the warrior springs out from his hunched position like a human trebuchet.

144

'He has a dagger!' I scream at the top of my voice. 'He still has a dagger.'

But too late. De Berclay has already seized the shocked young man and holds the rusty metal blade to his hostage's throat, pinning Colban Graham's arms behind his back.

'Safe passage! I demand safe passage,' the Commander shrieks like a demon possessed.

24

MAKE HASTE

Everyone has jumped back, but for reasons I will never be able to fathom, I do the opposite. De Berclay did not expect it—I know because when I smash into him sideways with the full force of my weight, he hadn't tensed his muscles in anticipation. He is flailing to regain his balance. I swing my arm against his knife handle and the weapon flies from his hand in an arch and lands at Sir Hector Graham's feet.

The Commander issues a curse and immediately seeks to close his strong hands around Squire Graham's throat instead, but Godfrey is a quick thinker and will not allow it. He launches himself at the Commander, grasps his arm and dangles his whole weight from the man's balled fist. When De Berclay tries to shake him off, the boy sinks his teeth into it. An angry yelp emanates from De Berclay's clenched lips. This gives Colban Graham the opportunity he needed to break free. In the blink of an eye, three English Knights have stepped up, pressing the tips of their swords to De Berclay's throat. Behind them, seven archers surround us, each bow tensed and ready to fire an arrow straight betwixt the Commander's eyes.

'Safe passage you shall have,' the Herald says. 'Safe passage to a dungeon. And then, if it pleases the King, to the gallows.'

Our Castle Commander's arms hang limp; his mouth slackens and even his eyes droop a little. Colban Graham rubs his throat and joins his people again.

Then, in a rattle of chainmail, seven or eight soldiers are upon De Berclay, obscuring him from view. There is a scuffle as he struggles one last time. Godfrey and I still stand in the same place, the eyes of all Caerlaverock's people on us, but once again, my head is filled with Fa and Fa alone.

The Old Sir Graham orders for De Berclay to be led away, stripped to his undergarments, bound and shackled. before advancing with his nephew. Now that I see them close up, their green velvet tabards are exquisitely trimmed with gold and embroidered with the family's crest: a falcon, ripping the heart out of a struggling stork.

'Uncle, this is Ada, a maid who aided me when my need was greatest. May God bless her.'

Our eyes meet. He will be a Knight; I am a maid. But

both our lives were endangered by that man's greed, and both our courage was required to thwart it. Insomuch, we are equal. But I can't return his smile, not yet. *Enough talking, enough waiting!* I drop to my knees. 'I prithee, may I return to the castle one more time? I am sure that the Commander overpowered my father to obtain his disguise. Oh, do not send me away. I know he is likely to be dead, but he is all I have left in the world.' At this, my voice breaks a little and Godfrey wordlessly slides onto his knees beside me to join my plight.

It takes messengers, and more waiting than my heart can endure. Finally, the permission comes. Followed by something like two hundred enemy soldiers who swarm like ants to make the castle secure in their favour, I sprint to the kitchen.

Godfrey's legs are shorter, so he gets there a couple of seconds after me. Fa isn't here, though there are blood splats on the flagstones—still red, not yet blackened by the air. *Oh, make haste. Where could he be?*

'Ada, look,' Godfrey whispers, hesitating. Now I see it too: there is a thin smear of blood leading to the scullery where the dry food is kept. Did De Berclay drag my father's stripped body there? In a couple of strides, I'm at the partition cloth and whip it back so hard it actually comes off its hooks. My head swims. An icy shiver travels from the very roots of my hair, to the small of my back, and the skin on my arms and legs prickles.

There he lies: the motionless bulk of my Fa. Without his apron, without his gloves, and without all of his knives which usually dangle from the belt around his waist. The angle at which he is sloped against the sacks looks so unnatural. Bile swells in my throat and I turn myself away. I simply cannot look on. I cannot.

Godfrey slowly advances and swallowing away what must be his own eight-year-old-fear, bends over my father's chest. Fa's face is hidden, and I'm too scared to look. *What has De Berclay done?*

'Ada,' Godfrey's voice is weak. He stretches a hand towards Fa, and there is blood on it when he retracts it.

'Ada… I think, I think he's…'

Dead. I know. He's dead, I know it. I am all alone in the world.

Godfrey's voice recovers and sounds stronger as he raises himself up. 'I think he's still breathing.'

A scream explodes from my mouth, so raw that it would rip the very back of my throat.

25

THE SCULLERY

I crouch beside my father who groans a little now.

'Fetch water, Godfrey. Be quick, I beg you, hurry.'

A crowd of soldiers has gathered outside the kitchen doorway and Colban Graham and his uncle stand with them. 'Let us help. There must a doctor with our army. Several, I'll wager,' the young man says before he disappears.

Doctor? The likes of us can't afford doctors! But he is already gone. With gentleness and care, I wipe my father's wound. The bleeding seems to have stopped, but he is pale, so very pale.

'Here, drink this.' Sir Hector Graham bends down and offers Fa a small vial from his gird. My hand twitches. I want to swat it away, even though I know he means well. I am simply so tightly wound and wish above all that life was simple again, just Fa and me. But there is something trustworthy in Sir Hector's voice and I accept his offer.

From behind, I feel a small hand on my back: Godfrey's. I am not alone. Even if the worst should happen, I shall not be alone.

It feels like an eternity, but eventually, my father swallows and groans, whether with pain or with relief, I cannot tell.

Footsteps clatter on the cobbles as more soldiers enter the castle.

'Let me through, I prithee. Let through the man of God to attend to the sick.'

It is Friar Malcolm.

'I begged leave to return to assist you. I know a little medicine.'

Old Graham raises his eyebrows. The Friar drops his gaze and amends: 'A very little… but I can pray.'

He turns Fa around and with Old Graham's help, creates a makeshift bed out of sacks and his grey habit. 'May St Lawrence intercede for him.'

The patron saint of all cooks. Of course.

The Friar, undaunted, removes Fa's garments around the cut and I shudder.

'It's not as bad as I thought, though he must surely have fainted with the sudden loss of blood.' The Friar's voice resumes a soothing tone, as if conducting a mass. 'Now, the four humours need to be restored: phlegm, yellow bile, black bile, and blood. The body's balance is crucial.'

We wait for him to do something. Anything.

'How do we do that?' I ask aloud, eventually.

He scratches his head. 'We bind up the wound as best as we can,' mumbles the Friar. 'After that, all we can do is pray.'

So that's exactly what we do.

26

TO WHITHORN

'That's him there, it must be!'

Godfrey points excitedly, but he simply cannot make his horse go faster, not with Fa sloped in the saddle and our bundles strapped on behind. The Friar's little dog, Nosewise, scampers along, disappearing into the long grass and re-emerging by the roadside, wagging his tail.

Godfrey was allowed to keep his clan tabard in the end, and proudly wears the De Heron Heraldry once more, ready to be reunited with his kin. Inch by inch, the distance shrinks and my humour mirrors the dark grey skies above. I should be grateful for the gift of the horse from the Graham clan so we could take Fa to the healing shrine of St Ninian. I should be glad of the Friar's company, so freely offered on our dismissal from Caerlaverock. I should be relieved that we are alive.

And yet.

The nobleman standing by the waymark-cross in

the distance could almost rival the Lord Maxwell in his splendour and stands relaxed as if there was nothing to be concerned about: no war, no border and no King.

He raises his hand in greeting.

'Grandfather!' Godfrey drops the reins of the horse which the Friar had allowed him to hold and runs towards the nobleman. They don't embrace like servants would. There is laughter though, and much clapping on Godfrey's shoulders, after the first brief bow.

I want the ground to swallow me up. In this world, beyond Caerlaverock and beyond the siege, Godfrey is of consequence. I am not. In good time, he will grow to have influence and I will not.

But the Almighty has ordained it so. No, what tortures me is this: I will miss my friend.

'Grandfather, you must meet Ada. She is the bravest person I know!'

The grey-haired Lord Heron is a little taken aback— he was going to exchange words with the Friar, but Godfrey insists, dragging the old man towards me. 'She saved my life. Don't look so incredulous, Grandfather, she really did, and more than once. Her father here was badly hurt—oh, I have *so* much to tell you. Are you well? God be praised. And Mother, is Mother well? I don't even know where to begin!'

Yes, that is the Godfrey I remember, before it all. I want to cry, but I can't help laughing too.

Thankfully, the old Lord Heron is a smiling man with easy manners who even slips the Friar an envelope, maybe to help with expenses.

'That reminds me,' the Friar exclaims, looking outraged with himself for a moment. 'The Lady Maxwell asked me to give you this, Ada. She said something about payment for good advice, although I may have misheard that.'

He retrieves a small velveteen parcel from the folds of his robe and presses it into my hand. I finger it nervously. There is something inside it, something small and round.

'Ada! It's the ring!' Godfrey and I take turns to hold in in awe, until I button the precious gift into the pouch on my belt and breathe a little deeper, steeling myself for the farewell.

'Godfrey.'

'I know.'

I look down on him and wish I had been granted a brother. Even a wild and proud one like this. He tilts his head upwards to mine and begins a bow, but something comes over me and I sweep him into an embrace so fierce that I knock him off his feet. I stagger a little to recover my balance.

'Godspeed, Godfrey. You'll make a brave and godly Knight one day. I'm just sorry that I won't be there to see it. I won't ever forget you.'

He hugs me back hard, despite his grandfather's

furrowed forehead.

'Godspeed, Ada. Until we meet again. I shall light all the candles I can afford for your father; I promise you that.'

Soon after, the Friar and I find ourselves back on the road. It can't be so very far now. Where better to beg healing for Fa than at the shrine of St Ninian?

The Friar leads the charger now, with my father slouched over it. What hardships that beast must have seen, what battles it must have endured! My humour is heavy with parting sorrow, but I pray all the harder.

During a roadside rest, I even persuade the Friar to hear my confession, and it feels good to hold nothing back for the first time I can remember. Fa rests against a tree, in a brief nap. I listen hard for the gurgling and rattling that can be the Herald of death, but I hear none; not yet at least. Through the course of the afternoon, I begin to hope: the wound has closed almost fully and is healing, I believe. I pray fervently to the Almighty, as I can't choose betwixt St Hunna—*don't leave this laundress fatherless, intercede for me*—and St Lawrence, patron saint of cooks—*don't allow him to die just yet. Save this cook from the fate of death before his time. Intercede for him.*

Again, and again, my fingers travel to my father's handiwork, the carved wooden image of St Hunna, patron saint of all laundresses, around my neck. It gives me comfort.

With Fa safely tucked up in bed at the inn at Whithorn, the Friar and I take a break in the courtyard in the dying hours of the day, watching the sun slide slowly into its watery grave. My heart is full, so full that I hardly notice the corners of the Friar's mouth drawing upwards, until he finally allows himself a smile so broad that I can't help teasing him. 'What is your news? You have not smiled thus for all the days the King of England has been in our lands.'

He chuckles. 'The world is not as I would have it, Ada, that much is true. But there are blessings, too. Blessings which may never have come to us without the hardships. Like this.'

He slides a hand into his grey habit and produces an opened letter.

I recognise it. 'The Lord Heron gave you that, Godfrey's kin. I recognise the seal. Is it money?'

'It is better than money.' His smile holds. 'It is peace of mind, whatever happens.'

I raise my eyebrows.

'You see, Ada, I will have to return to Greyfriars in Dumfries. It's where I belong, especially now. I fear proper peace in these lands is still a long way off.'

My head sinks onto my chest, but I know he is right. *What of the place where I belong? Caerlaverock is the only home I have ever known, but I cannot return there.* 'Do not fear for me, Friar,' I say with half-hearted confidence. 'My father will live, and we will—'

'Exactly!' he interrupts. 'Now I do *not* fear for you anymore. Because in this envelope, Ada, is your future. The Lord Heron wrote a letter of recommendation. He says that if you find yourself uncertain of your position, a laundress is always needed in his family. He writes that they should be honoured to employ a cook of such quality and reputation as your father—why, they would be the envy on both sides of the border.' The Friar chuckles. 'He urges you, whatever happens at the shrine, to return and seek out Castle Heron where you will be treated well.'

I can't speak, so the Friar fills the silence for me.

'Ada, the question of your future was what troubled me the most. My soul is light now. My prayers have been heard. Praise be.'

He rises and enters the inn again, just as the golden glow above the water evaporates and a chill settles on the courtyard. Through the door, I can hear the innkeeper's wife scraping the ash pan and stacking new wood in the grate. Here in the open air, plovers' and terns' cries swirl above the splash of each new wave.

But there is a different sound too.

Oh Lord, oh Lord, there is another sound I'd know anywhere in the world. A sound I love more than life itself.

Through the open window above us, 'tis the sound of Fa singing.

Singing!

I smile.

And then I laugh. I raise my eyes up through my tears. Above me, the sky has exploded into orange and purple, with a flock of skylarks dancing a reel with the clouds.

THE END

GLOSSARY

Armoury—place where weapons are kept

Barter—exchange of goods or services

Breastplate—piece of armour covering the chest

Broadsword—sword with a double-edged, wide blade

Burgess—free citizen of a burgh

Burgh—market town

Castle Commander—man in charge of castle defences

Catapult—war device used to throw objects at high speed over a great distance *(see also Trebuchet)*

Chainmail—armour made of linked metal rings

Chambers—rooms; living quarters

Chivalry—code followed by Knights where courage, honour and kindness are important

Clan—group of families, who originally came from the same family and have the same name

Coat of arms—special symbol that is the sign of a family; used by Knights on their seal and armour

Cold-store—cold cellar where food is kept fresh

Crusades—religious war fought by Christians

Curtain wall—wall surrounding a castle enclosure

Death knell—ringing of a bell to mark someone's death

Dirk—small pointed knife or dagger (Scottish)

Drawbridge—bridge that can be raised or brought down to protect a castle from attack

Dungeon—room or cell in which prisoners are held, especially underground

Ell—old unit of measurement for cloth; combined length of the forearm and extended hand

Feud—prolonged and bitter quarrel or dispute, especially between families

Gaberlunzies—beggars

Guild—a group of craftsmen of a specific trade or craft such as making shoes or weaving cloth

Herald—messenger

Hose—clothes worn on the legs, similar to trousers

Ingot—piece of brick-shaped metal; often silver or gold

Kin—family and relative(s)

Lady—wife to a ruler/master

Laundress—servant who washes clothes and linen

League—an old distance measurement, roughly 5.5km

Lord—ruler/master and the holder of a castle

Mead—alcoholic drink made from honey and water

Mercat Cross—market cross, a symbolic monument in the centre of a market town

Midsummer Feast—usually celebrated on 24th June; also known as St John's Day

Moat—ditch around a castle filled with water; Caerlaverock Castle had two moats

Page—young boy who acts as a servant for a Knight, while training to become a Knight

Parchment—thin, dried animal skin used for writing on

Parley—to discuss terms with the opposing side

Portcullis—strong gate made of bars with points at the bottom; hangs above castle entrance and is brought down to close the entrance to enemies

Pit prison—underground dungeon

Range—kitchen fireplace where food was prepared

Reivers—raiders along the Scottish/English border

Relic—part of the body (such as a bone) or something that belonged to a saint

Scullion—servant given the lowliest kitchen tasks

Sentry—soldier who stands guard

Serf—servant

Shift—medieval dress; worn under skirts and aprons

Siege engine—weapon used to destroy fortifications or castle walls such as battering ram or trebuchet

Siege tower—mobile wooden tower used to transfer troops onto a wall

Squire—Knight in training who would take care of the Knight's armour and weapons, and accompany the Knight into battle

Tabard—short coat worn by men in the Middle Ages

Toll—charge to enter a burgh or cross a bridge

Toun—cluster of buildings outside the castle walls

Trebuchet—type of catapult (*see also* **Catapult**)

Visor—part of a helmet which protected the face

Wimple—medieval head-covering for women

View of entrance to Caerlaverock Castle

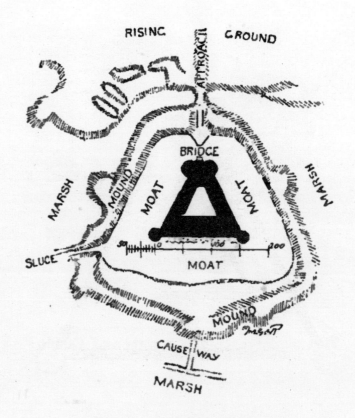

Caerlaverock Castle Site Plan

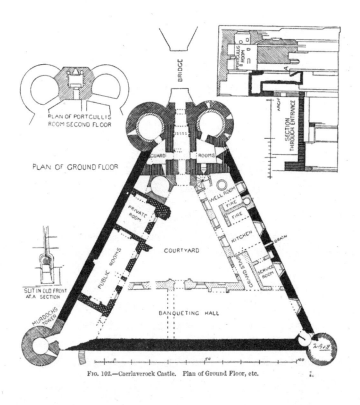

PLAN OF PORTCULLIS
ROOM SECOND FLOOR

PLAN OF GROUND FLOOR

SLIT IN OLD FRONT
AT A SECTION

FIG. 102.—Caerlaverock Castle. Plan of Ground Floor, etc.

Caerlaverock Castle Ground Floor Plan

SCOTTISH WARS OF INDEPENDENCE TIMELINE

c1270 William Wallace is born. His father was respectable, but not part of the Royal family.

1274 (11 July) Robert Bruce is born at Turnberry Castle in Ayrshire. He is related to the Scots, Gaelic and English Royal families.

1286 The old King of Scots, Alexander III, falls from his horse and is killed. The next in line to the throne is three-year-old Margaret, known as the 'Maid of Norway.'

1290 Margaret, Maid of Norway, falls ill during her sea voyage from Norway to Scotland and dies in Orkney.

1292 John Balliol becomes King of Scots.

1294 The English King Edward Longshanks wants the Scots to join him in his war against the French. Instead, France and Scotland agree to help each other against England. Edward prepares to make war on Scotland.

1296 Edward's army invades Scotland and defeats the Scots at Dunbar. John Balliol is captured and imprisoned in the Tower of London.
The Scots are ordered to 'swear fealty', to sign a letter supporting Edward. Neither William Wallace nor Robert Bruce sign it. Wallace becomes outlawed.

1296 The Stone of Destiny is taken to England. William Wallace leads a rebellion.

1297 William Wallace beats Edward's army.

1298 Edward's army beats Wallace's army.

1300 The Siege of Caerlaverock takes place.

1304 Wallace is now a fugitive as other Scots start giving up and supporting Edward.

1305 Wallace is betrayed and killed.

1306 Robert Bruce fights his rival at Greyfriars Kirk in Dumfries.

1306 Robert Bruce is made King of Scots. But a surprise dawn attack means Bruce only just escapes. He becomes a fugitive. Bruce's wife, his sisters and his daughter are imprisoned by Edward Longshanks. However, the King is ill.

1307 King Edward Longshanks dies and is replaced by his much weaker son, Edward II.

1314 Bruce's well-trained forces defeat Edward II's army at Bannockburn. Bruce's family is returned to him.

1320 Bruce is in power.

In the Declaration of Arbroath, the powerful people in Scotland say:

'It is not for glory, nor for riches, nor honours that we are fighting, but for freedom itself, which no honest person gives up but with life itself.'

AUTHOR'S NOTE

I remember the day I first set foot in Caerlaverock Castle. It was a damp, muddy, drizzly and grey Dumfries-shire day and my kids were mutinous. I had dragged them to beautiful Dumfries and Galloway on a brief Easter break. The *real* reason, of course was that I was researching one of my other books, *Black Water*, and I needed to check the lie of the land. We stayed in a remote farmhouse—the rain and the mud, oh my goodness!

It was a Friday. The weather looked as grim as the preceding days and we needed to get out of the house, this much was clear. Caerlaverock Castle was a short drive away. 'We're going to a castle.' I announced.

My answer came in the form of three teenage groans from beneath duvets. Half an hour later we were on our way.

And this is the beauty of a story! It assails you when you least expect it. My head was in another book altogether; I was not looking for a new idea. And yet, I walked into the exhibition and saw the siege missiles displayed—huge spheres of rock I could barely imagine flying through the air, and I was smitten. All but forgotten was everything I had ever worked on before—I *had* to write *this* book, about *this* siege. I took photographs of every display board and ordered a copy of the heraldic poem which described those heady days in the year 1300.

The truth is, I have long been fascinated by all things medieval. The poem became dog-eared in my hands. How could I make my story stand out from the crowd? A female perspective, yes, that was new. Ada was born, feisty and moral and brave. But there was so much I didn't know!

I discovered that women were never cooks in the Middle Ages. Castle cooks were men! Who knew? I unearthed that the named Commander of Caerlaverock was killed in a battle at Lochmaben just a few months before the events described in the book. Who could have replaced him? There was no record, so I was free to create my own villain within the castle walls. And a prisoner could have been taken during that confrontation, I supposed. There was a record of a pit-prison at Caerlaverock, so Colban Graham entered my tale. Unexpectedly fascinating details were around every research corner—the Clan Maxwell history, the heraldic symbols, the regimented training for Knights, Squires and Pages, burgh markets and border raids. In addition, I discovered that high-ranking ladies and monks were the most likely to own pets, and that the most common name for a cat was 'Gilbert'. Dogs often had descriptive names, and of the ones I found 'Nosewise' appealed to me the most.

Joking aside, it must have been a very unsettling time to live in. With the brutal King Edward Longshanks in charge in England, William Wallace defeated and on the run, and with other successors squabbling for power, the Maxwells must have agonised over their allegiance—whom should they support? Raids and feuds were common and life was cheap, particularly a servant girl's.

I have thoroughly enjoyed Ada's and Godfrey's company in the writing of this book and I miss them terribly already.

Just as well that other ideas assail me when I least expect it to happen!

I hope that the charm of Caerlaverock Castle captures you too. Its name means 'Fort of the Skylarks'. Perhaps you'll have the chance to visit and see it for yourself.

And maybe your imagination can soar there, like mine did.

ACKNOWLEDGEMENTS

First off, huge thanks to Anne and Iain Glennie of Cranachan Publishing, who are unfailingly supportive and constructive, and to the whole of #ClanCranachan! Thank you to Sandra McGowan for the incredible illustrations and to my SCBWI family and the Inverness children's writers on whom I tested early snippets of this book.

My most heartfelt thanks must go to Dr Lucy Dean of the University of the Highland and Islands Centre for History. I made contact out of the blue and offered to buy her lunch to ask my motley collection of random medieval research questions. If she wasn't sure of an answer, she asked other medievalists and forwarded me their replies in a constant stream of Twitter messages. Particular thanks also to Dr Iain MacInnes of UHI Centre for History for his input.

Thanks to Historic Environment Scotland for their excellent publications and resources which clarified many a conundrum.

And as always, thank you to my Carla, Isla and Duncan for being my companions in my story quests, and to Rob, for everything, always. I thank God for you every day.